W9-CPM-458

JaCAraNDa

JaCAraNDa

Cherie Priest

SUBTERRANEAN PRESS 2015

First Edition

ISBN
978-1-59606-684-7

Subterranean Press
PO Box 190106
Burton, MI 48519

subterraneanpress.com

Part One

The Nun

Galveston Island, Texas. 1895

THE NUN'S LETTER INTERCEPTED JUAN Miguel Quintero Rios on the road to Port Bolivar. Her handwriting was small and precise, and easy to read—even in the back of a bouncing cart on a rough-paved road made rougher by the lunging wind. No natural-born American, that one. Irish, the padre guessed by her name and her habit. What she was doing on the Gulf was anyone's guess, and how she'd learned of him, he did not know; it was the only question she left unanswered in her carefully composed response.

He did not care, but he was curious.

Despite that one omission, her small bundle of papers contained a wealth of new information. At first she'd told him only that the hotel hated, and it hungered. Now, in this most recent message, she told him the rest.

In 1878, a cattle baron by the name of Jack Darnell had bought the property and its surrounding acreage, hoping to

Cherie Priest

build a resort that would rival any in Houston—or even the great estates of the Caribbean. But his plans were hotly resisted by the locals, for in order to create this "castle on an island," a landmark must be destroyed.

On the site of the proposed hotel, a blue jacaranda bloomed.

No one knew for certain why the tree was planted there, or who had installed it on the island—though someone must have done so, for it was not native to the region; and it was quite ancient by any standard. Alas, the original gardener had long since passed, leaving no real clues behind.

But one rumor had attained the status of a fairy tale, short and sad: A conquistador loved a woman, and that woman had loved the jacaranda. When she died, he planted this one in her honor, if not her memory—for not even the most dedicated listener or oldest island resident knew the woman's name.

And after all, that was only a rumor.

(Though it might have held a grain of truth, it just as likely didn't.)

Regardless, the tree was greatly beloved. For as long as anyone remembered, it had been a favorite place for lovers to meet and children to climb. Its trumpet-shaped flowers cascaded in clusters of purple-blushed indigo; over the years they'd been woven into the braids of a thousand maidens, and offered in a thousand gestures of romantic intent. They were gathered into bouquets for weddings, and laid upon caskets as sweet farewells. To be sure, there were other flowers on the island, but none compared to these.

All the same, ground was broken for Jack Darnell's hotel.

And likewise was the tree.

People came from every corner of the island to witness its destruction, not with the morbid glee of those who attend a hanging—but with the sorrow of a loved one's wake. It was said that one last blossom was taken in the end, and pressed between the pages of a Methodist minister's bible...as a reminder of the wickedness that men may do.

Wicked or only ambitious, Darnell constructed his castle.

He never gave a second thought to the tree; in fact, he had never set eyes on it in the first place.

Whereas the tree had been living, lithe, and sprawling, the hotel that replaced it was a blocky, almost manly affair—built in a style just ahead of its time, or so Darnell was assured by his architects. Its symmetry was clean and precise, and its lines stopped short of being austere, for there were touches of art at the corners, and details of refinement along the ivory plaster and red bricks, the graphite shade of the cornerstones and the wood-framed windows, with their narrow sills and shutters the color of rust. Inside, the floors were set with clean, dramatic mosaic tiles in sharp white, black, and green; and the fixtures were mostly brass that had been polished until they gleamed like mirrors.

It spoke of wealth without too much ostentation, and quality without excessive frivolity. All in all, it was a restrained place for a man with so much money and such grandiose plans, but his wife might have been the guiding, stabilizing hand in that matter.

In the end, the hotel was given her name. They called it *Odessa's Court.*

The padre wondered what sort of name "Odessa" was, and where it might have come from. Perhaps he'd ask when he arrived, and maybe someone would know.

A gust of wind tugged at the letter; he held its pages tightly until the bluster passed. Above, the sky was going pale, all the blue washed out of it. A storm was coming. Or rather, he was coming toward a storm.

He read on, picking up the tale on the next sheet.

The millionaire and his bride were the hotel's first two victims.

Jack Darnell was found hanging in the lobby, dangling from one of the new-fashioned fans with tracks that snaked along the ceiling. Though dead, he moved slowly, back and forth across the room, drawn along by the ratcheting chain—his feet dangling ten feet off the floor. Odessa Darnell lay face-down on the ground beneath him, her skull shattered against the tiles by what must have been a terrible fall from the second story landing.

The Texas Rangers called it a double suicide. The case was closed, and in the wake of three more deaths in the span of a month…so was the hotel.

For fourteen years it sat empty, until it was purchased by a private investment group in San Antonio. A manager was sent out to assess the property, and upon his approval everything was cleaned, renovated, and re-opened under a new name: the *Jacaranda Hotel*, after the long-gone landmark.

The nun suggested that this was a canny move, or else a superstitious one. It would seem that they hoped to appease whatever unhappy thing had taken up residence there.

At any rate, according to Sister Eileen, the former republic (and now mere state) of Texas was sending a Ranger to investigate, or so it'd vowed—but no such man had yet arrived. In all frankness, she did not expect her request to be taken very seriously by anyone in Austin. It was too hard to frame the problem while leaving out all the stranger, stickier bits. She had to tell them that people were dying, yes. She was compelled to admit they died by storm, by suicide, by accident, and by coincidence: almost two dozen of them, in singles and in clusters. She was bound to confess they'd been unable to uncover any murderer, or even any plot of murder.

She requested their intervention all the same, with all haste, before the tally of dead could rise any higher.

But she knew—she *believed*—she could tell the padre everything else...the whole truth, so help her God. Even if Texas would not answer, *he* might.

He finished her letter a full hour before he finished his journey, arriving at Port Bolivar just as the first spits and hisses of rain began to fall. The sky was still white, the curdled color of milk on the verge of turning.

The grain driver dropped him off at the pier, where they parted on friendly terms. The padre was grateful for the ride. The driver was grateful for having shared a confession so minor, that it was a wonder it'd weighed upon his heart so heavily, and for so long.

With a round of thanks, the padre set off for the ferry.

"You're a madman, you know," the driver called out as he cracked the reigns to get his horse's attention. "Everyone with any sense is leaving Galveston, before it's washed away."

2

THE PADRE ROAMED FREELY ALONG the small ferry's deck. He avoided the maintenance men and the wheel operators, the carts stacked with seeds and flour and other supplies, and the soft stampings of anxious horses who'd much rather swim than float. He did not need to avoid the other passengers, for there weren't any.

At first he paced, back and forth from stern to prow beneath the overhang to keep himself and his satchel dry; and then he settled on a quiet spot where he could watch the Gulf in peace. It did not quite churn, but it rumbled, and its low waves were frothed with spittle. The water was as gray as the sky was white.

Finally, a long line of land came into view: a shadow as thick as the width of his finger, then his thumb, and then he could pick out the details—pale strips of sand, clusters of trees, great fluffy tufts of sea oats fattening the banks at high tide.

As the ferry drew up close to its pier, Rios saw the men who worked the simple dock with its accompanying row of warehouses and businesses. Big-shouldered fellows lifted crates alone, or with the help of others; well-dressed women observed from a deck up above the water, pointing and whispering behind gloved hands. Dogs barked, greeting the incoming craft. Cats hung closer to the fishing boats and small pools left by the receding waves, trying their paws at crab-catching and shrimp stealing—all the while competing with circling bands of chattering seagulls, hoping to snatch their own meals from the water or the shore.

The day was warm, but not unreasonably so for May—and the ocean breeze blew damp and chilly with the not-quite-rain when the craft was tied into place, a ramp dropped down onto the deck, and the padre was allowed to arrive.

Everyone else was leaving.

As soon as he'd descended the ramp, Galveston residents climbed it. One by one they boarded the ferry and dropped their fares into the captain's box; and one by one they stepped onto the wet, sun-bleached boards of the dock.

The padre had never been to the island before, but he knew it wasn't large. He had a map, borrowed from a friend back in Houston, and the map had precious little upon it—save a half dozen streets, a park or two, and a notation with regards to the churches, a convent, and a prison.

The Jacaranda Hotel was marked with a penciled-in "x."

He set off on foot. The distance wasn't more than a couple of miles, and he was ready to move his legs after all the riding and sailing. Besides, the scenery was pleasant, the rain was mostly holding off, and the roads were not so bad. Some stretches were paved, and some were long expanses of chalk-white sand and gray-swirled dirt, pocked with little wads of tar that washed in with the ocean.

There was no sun, but the air was tangy, familiar, and welcoming.

Not so the Jacaranda Hotel.

It wasn't visible through the trees, and indeed it was utterly concealed until he stood directly before it; there were only three stories, and the roof was flat—in the tradition of places that fear the shearing forces of an occasional hurricane. The structure was not precisely squat but long and blocky, brick and plaster, with hints of imported stone. It was made of reds and whites that had faded under the coastal sun, and now appeared to be browns and creams.

Two oversized doors made of carved oak waited beneath a great black canopy, up a short series of stairs.

Juan Miguel Quintero Rios stood still, and listened.

Gulls shrieked greedily back and forth, squirrels scurried and scattered, and shorebirds called their softer, sweeter calls back and forth to one another. Out on the water a loud, low whistle blew, so another ferry was either coming or going, signaling to the lighthouse at the island's southernmost point.

He listened harder.

Under his feet the sandy earth shifted as moles, rats, and snakes cut their passages from place to place; the men at the docks dropped freight as heavy as mules, rattling the pier and startling the stray cats. Beyond the far edge of the horizon, clouds whispered against each other, coiled up, and collected together. Butterflies flapped their feather-light wings and dusted the bright pink azaleas.

He closed his eyes.

Bricks settled and shifted, cornerstones grumbled. The great oak doors swelled and shrank in their frames. Below, much farther down than the oil-specked sands or the paved, angled walkways that flanked the hotel and led to its gardens, something enormous and very dark rolled over.

It turned, restless as a fevered sleeper. It did not breathe or whisper, but it moaned. It hummed. It *growled*.

Cherie Priest

***

He opened his eyes. Snapped them open, only to narrow them again at the curved black canopy and the doors beneath it.

"So there you are," he said.

But nothing answered.

The padre adjusted his satchel, sliding the strap up higher on his shoulder. Despite the breeze and the damp he was warm from the walk, and a bit uncomfortable though there was no sun to bake his black cassock (which was only made of cotton, anyway).

He put one foot forward, and felt only a very slight, very faint resistance...so he took another step. Feeling resistance there too, he pressed harder next time. Kicking against something thick and unwilling, below the earth itself. Left foot, right foot, pushing against whatever waited inside, underneath.

Against whatever did not want him there.

By the time he reached the steps, he was almost smiling. The hotel would have to do better than that, if it wanted him gone. The growl and the unwelcoming start did not frighten him. They only told him how much attention he ought to pay, and how frightened he might wish to be later.

But not yet.

The main door knockers were round and ornate, cast with decorative jacaranda blossoms at the top. A nice touch, he thought. He lifted one, then changed his mind and reached for the lever instead, opening the door to let himself inside.

The lobby was bright and clean.

A sweeping pair of staircases made a statement and an arc, leading to a mezzanine at the top, from whence the late Mrs. Darnell had no doubt fallen some years ago. The padre looked up at the ceiling and saw the fans turning, roaming on their

18

tracks. Three at a time on each side of the room, trundling back and forth like toy trains, to keep the air moving. Their chains clacked together like teeth.

Yes, this was where the Darnells had died.

But when he listened, he heard only a stain: a gargling sound and a crash, and the dribbling noise of blood collecting into a pool. He did not hear any anger, any hatred. He heard no murder, only death.

A great desk and a long counter awaited him along the far wall, and behind them was a mirror—the sort he'd seen behind bars, in the occasional saloon…back when he'd frequented such places. It had been awhile, but not so long that he suspected the style had changed.

In the mirror he met own eyes, and then he looked elsewhere.

He saw a young woman in a crisp blue dress, ready to hear his name and give him a room if he'd only sign the guest book and arrange his payment. He saw the fans running along the ceiling, performing their mechanical ballet back and forth, back and forth. He saw the gleam of the floor and the fixtures, and an elevator he hadn't noticed at first.

He looked harder.

There was a blur, a flash of arms and legs and blood, falling. Crashing. Falling again, in a cycle as true as the fans above him. No sound at all. Only the shape, the impression of flailing and fear, horror and the quick, messy shine of brains on tiles. And up there, another shadow. A smudge with less definition than a thumbprint. Riding along the tracks, keeping company with the roving, mindless fans.

He blinked. He blinked again, scrubbing the images away.

The young woman behind the counter smiled at him. "Can I help you?"

He stepped forward and placed his satchel on the floor beside his feet. "I would like a room."

"Very good!" she exclaimed. She was surprised, but glad. And something else, but he wasn't listening hard anymore, so he couldn't tease it out. "How long will you be staying with us? A few days at least, I should think—until the storm has passed. I don't think it will be too bad, but you never do know."

"I hope you are right. And yes, I will stay a few days."

All of this in English, for nothing about the woman suggested she knew a word of Spanish. His words vibrated softly with an accent, but he was easy enough to understand. Only the occasional fool pretended otherwise.

When he gave the girl his name, she made another small exclamation: "Oh! I have a message for you. It's from Sister Eileen. She said you'd be joining us." From under the desk she retrieved an envelope, folded but not sealed. It said "Father Rios" in handwriting he now found familiar.

He thanked her, but he did not open it yet.

The woman, whose name was Sarah, gave him a room key in exchange for three days' worth of board. She retrieved a paper sign that said, "Back in 5 minutes." She took him to the elevator and drew back its cage. She stepped inside, inviting him to do likewise.

"It's a new addition," she explained. "The owners had it installed a month ago. It's lovely, don't you think?"

"A fine device," he agreed. Its buttons were glass, and indicated the three visible floors as well as a basement. The floor was tiled with large black and white squares of linoleum that felt firm but spongy when he bounced slightly on his heels. A glass bulb in a metal cage cast out light from a vivid yellow filament; it flickered when the girl pulled a lever, and the lift began to rise.

"You'll be on the third floor on the north wing. Same wing as Sister Eileen, though she's on the second floor. Shall I tell her you've arrived?"

"No, do not bother her."

The elevator climbed smoothly, and when the third level landing presented itself, Sarah pulled the lever again—lining up the floors for a seamless exit. "As you like. Please, make yourself comfortable. If you need anything, I'll be downstairs. Or you can ring from your room," she told him. "The bell will bring me or one of the Alvarez ladies, right away."

"Thank you, but I have had a long week's journey. I will need some rest, and to refresh myself."

He did not intend to rest, but he did not want the young woman's company, either.

3

THE PADRE PUT HIS SATCHEL on the foot of the bed, and sat down beside it. The envelope from the nun was crisp and insistent in his pocket, so he opened it with his thumb and extracted the contents: a single sheet of plain paper. It read, "You can find me in room 203. We have so much to talk about."

Though his travels had been uneventful, they were tiring all the same...but she was right, they had much to talk about. And below his feet he could feel (without even listening) the rumbling churn of something that was not very happy to have him here. That was fine with him. He wasn't happy to be there, but he knew where he was needed. It could fuss and grumble all it wanted.

He went to the basin and splashed some water on his face, toweled himself off, and left his bag sitting on the bed.

Room 203 was downstairs, but he preferred to skip the elevator.

Cherie Priest

He walked a long carpet runner that went the length of the hallway, and noted gaslamp fixtures at regular intervals, keeping the area bright despite the lack of windows. At the end of the wing, closest to the elevator, he also spied a heavy, enormous fire door on a great hinge—a feature that was quite common, even in buildings as forward-thinking as this one. Fire does not care for architecture. It hungers for whatever it can find, and when there isn't enough water to douse it, there's nothing to be done except contain it and hope it dies. Close the great metal doors and seal off the flames. Let the fire consume all its own air, and suffocate.

Just beyond these doors, he found a set of stairs.

Down them he climbed, and on the second floor he strolled until he found number 203. He knocked, and within the room he heard the shuffling sound of someone roused from a seated position, as well as brief, hurried footsteps.

Sister Eileen Callahan opened the door with caution.

And then a smile.

The nun with precise, pretty handwriting was a full head smaller than the padre; her hair was mostly hidden by her gray and white head covering, but a ginger curl escaped—accompanied by a wisp of gray—and her eyes were the color of burnt caramel, gold and brown. She could have been anywhere between thirty and fifty years old, and Rios was far too polite to speculate. Hers was an ageless sort of face, and neither pretty nor plain, narrow nor plump. She stood before him with the competent air of a woman who is very often expected to know things and do things—immediately, and correctly.

"Hello, Father Rios." Her accent cemented his suspicions. Irish, though she'd been in the Americas for quite some time, he guessed. He guessed something else, too...even though he wasn't looking or listening. There was something else about her, some other foreign thing, distant and perhaps quite dark, but leashed for the time being.

It intrigued him, but didn't bother him. If there was something strange about her, that was just one more thing they had in common. It might even be why she summoned him. "Hello, Sister Eileen."

"I hope your trip was safe and pleasant."

"Safe enough. Pleasant enough."

"Good, because your time here at the hotel will not be." She stepped into the hall, and closed the door behind herself. "Here, won't you come with me? Let us walk together."

He welcomed the suggestion. The hotel was growing darker inside—maybe because the day was growing long, or the storm was coming closer, or he wasn't wanted there. He was careful not to listen, and not to look. He deliberately put those senses away, lest he intrude by accident on the wrong party.

He fell into step beside the small woman.

She led the way. He led the questions.

"I must ask, you understand: How did you learn of me?"

"Rumors, mostly." She, too, eschewed the elevator, in favor of the stairs. "You see things, you hear things. You know how it goes."

"I do," he murmured. He stood aside, and allowed her to proceed first.

Her voice carried up behind her, along with the barest hint of footsteps. "Stories travel faster than the telegraph codes, faster than magic if the stories are good enough. And yours are very good."

"You're too kind. Or too trusting of your sources," he demurred.

"Neither one, I assure you. I first heard of your adventures in Juarez, through a young woman who survived the outbreak there." She emerged on the first floor, and he joined her, stepping into the light that streamed in through the lobby windows. It was going pink—a coastal sunset the color of a shell's belly. "She said that you saved her. She said you saved them all."

"My role in that matter might have been overstated."

"It might have been. But then I heard of your encounter at the hospital in Albuquerque. And the incident at Rose Hill, late last year."

"Three isolated coincidences."

"Or a pattern," she countered. "One I'd be foolish to ignore, despite your objections. Particularly once I heard how you handled the rancher at Four Chairs." She lowered her voice. "They found parts of the creature on both sides of the West Texas line. It was a masterful handling."

"It was…a tricky affair, but it was resolved to everyone's satisfaction. Though I cannot guess *exactly* what you heard; I know how details are distorted in the retelling."

She stopped in the center of the lobby, between the staircase landings. Her small feet were planted at the edge of the large tile mosaic that decorated the floor there. The padre only just then realized that it was a swirling, blossoming pattern. It was less like a jacaranda flower, and more like a sunflower. No, that wasn't quite right either. This was something else, then. A design for the sake of design, and not a depiction of anything at all.

No. That was also wrong.

The nun watched him keenly, as he watched the patterns on the floor. "Guess whatever you want," she said. "I know what you are, and I know what you can do. I know this place needs someone like you, because God knows the Texans don't have the first idea how to handle what's happened here."

"Texans? I thought they were Texians, by their own preference."

"They were Texians when they were a nation. Now they're merely Texans." She lowered her voice, and winked as though there were some conspiracy in the matter. "But don't call them that, not to their faces. They don't like the reminder."

He tried to keep from smiling, and succeeded only in hiding his teeth. "I expect they don't. But it's far from the worst they might be called."

Sister Eileen relaxed her smile until it faded away. "I know. I know there's been so much tension between your nations. But you've come here to help, despite it all. I knew you would."

"My nation remains in doubt. No one can agree where the Mexico line was drawn in the first place, where it wandered over the century, or where it is located right this moment. I trust that one day, everyone will come to some agreement. Until then, I keep both sets of papers." It was a question he tired of answering. "Besides, there are more important things than borders. More dangerous things than armies and mapmakers."

She murmured some soft assent. "Indeed, and beneath our feet, even as we stand here admiring the trappings of a rich man's whims...there waits something much more awful than war." She paused. "Everything is large here in Texas, they take great pride in it. Well, they're right about the haint that makes this place its home, and they shouldn't be proud in the slightest. It should fill them all with horror."

He could hear it again, even though he wasn't really listening—or he surely didn't mean to. It throbbed below the floors, something huge, heavy, and slow. A pulse like the heartbeat of something so enormous, so great, that it must be the size of the great round Gulf itself. "If they had any sense, they'd burn this place to the ground and salt the earth, never to return."

The nun said something in reply, but he didn't catch it.

He begged her pardon.

She nodded, but her eyes were worried. "I said, they'll never do any such thing. Not while they think there's money to be made. It's the way of the world." She sighed. "Greed isn't quite the original sin, but I'd call it a younger sibling."

"That's perilously close to blasphemy, Sister…"

The worry drained from her eyes, to be replaced with something harder. "I've danced nearer to blasphemy before, and so have you. Something tells me, you're no more entitled to your vestments than I am mine."

Again he begged her pardon. "My apologies. It was a weak attempt at humor. I should have restrained myself."

She sighed, and rubbed at her eyes. "No, the apologies should be mine. My own self-restraint is insufficient; I mustn't cast stones. But here, you see where we are?" she changed her tone and the subject at once, indicating the lobby around them.

He followed her gesture, taking in the tiles with their dizzying patterns, and the tin ceiling tiles between the fan tracks—embossed with something more organic than the tiny squares that made up the shapes on the floor. The curved staircases in a sweeping pair. The elevator nestled to the left of them, its brass cage slid to the side, all angles and darkness within.

Only then did he notice that they were alone.

Sarah was not at the desk, and now there was no sign to indicate when or if she might return. The afternoon was dying and the gaslamps hissed on, one by one, so the light changed color—but did not leave them altogether.

"Where is everyone?" he asked the nun.

"Anywhere but here, I assume. They may not know the particulars, but no one wants to be alone under this roof. And especially, no one wants to be right *here*."

She tapped the edge of the mosaic with the toe of her plain black boot. Then she used her foot to point at the center, to a dark dot of marble the size of a dinner plate.

"I doubt the architects and artists knew that the tree ever stood here. They could not have designed this with such

precision. No, they were guided. The thing in this hotel...
it remakes itself. It..." she struggled to find the words. "It re-
draws itself, piece by piece—or it tried. It was a tree, it was
alive. It twisted and flowed, and bent in the wind. But now
it's been supplanted by this place, so huge and square—such a
block of boxes, stacked together. Nothing natural in here at all,
except the wood that was cut and polished for the handrails, the
doors, and the desk...but that's not the shape it wanted. So it
made another one for itself...it told them..."

She stared down at the floor and traced her toes in circles
along the lines; and the padre felt the same thing, some spiral,
drawing down. Water draining out of a tub. That pattern of a
dust devil. The turning of the earth, of a storm, of sand.

He finished for her. "It told them it looked like *this*."

She looked up suddenly, as if she was startled to hear his
voice. "Yes. So this is the only part that remains, the only thing
that looks like what it means. This is...this is..." She stepped
away, outside the pattern on the floor.

She stared at it from the edge, seeing the whole thing instead
of its pieces. "This is the shape of its soul."

SARAH RETURNED, AND FOUND THE pair of them standing by the great mosaic that spiraled both directions at once. She smiled broadly, the social smile of a woman who is paid to make it. "Oh, excellent—I see you two have found one another."

The nun smiled back, a similar expression with less contrived cheer, and more steady reasonableness. "Yes, dear. Thank you for sharing my message. I don't suppose any new telegrams have arrived...?"

"No ma'am, nothing new since yesterday."

"Ah, well. Any word about the weather, out of Houston?"

"Only that the storm is coming, and it should make landfall soon. They say we should evacuate if we can—but if we don't, everything will probably be all right."

The padre glanced out the nearest window and knew that the men in Houston were understating the matter, or perhaps the delay between telegrams and Mother Nature had gotten the best of them. The edge of the bone-white sky was tinged with purple, and a haze in the distance hinted that the horizon ushered something large and unpleasant towards shore.

It was still quite distant, just a smudge on the cusp of the world. Maybe the worst would not fall tonight. Maybe it'd find them tomorrow, or the day after.

But soon.

The nun may or may not have known the signs; the padre didn't know how versed she was, in the ways of coastal weather. She accepted the answer gracefully, as if it didn't matter either way. "That's good to hear. And one last thing, Sarah—if you'd be so kind as to indulge me: Is there any news from the Rangers?"

Sarah's smile slipped; it cracked at the edge, and for a small, short moment, it looked a little bit desperate. "None yet, I'm afraid. You *do* think they'll send someone, don't you? After what became of the Pattersons?"

"I'm quite certain they will." And now the nun was lying, if only with intent to comfort. He knew it in his bones.

"The Pattersons?"

"I'll explain before supper," she told him. "Speaking of which, Sarah? Is it served in the community room again?"

"Yes ma'am. We haven't yet finished...*you know*...so meals will be taken in the community room until further notice. I hope we'll have everything refreshed and restored by tomorrow, but you never can tell." She brightened again, and added, "At any rate, supper is served in half an hour. Until then, you're welcome to make yourself comfortable. Take some tea or coffee, as you like."

"Thank you, Sarah. We'll find our way there—after I finish showing Father Rios around the premises, if you don't mind."

"Do you mean to show him...the dining hall?"

"I do. But don't look at me like that," she chided gently. "Do not be afraid of his reaction. The father is here to help, just as I am."

"By all means," she said, but her faith in this matter did not seem particularly strong. She struggled to muster it, flashing a worried glance between the padre and the nun. "Father, you may as well know it: We need all the help we can get." With that, she withdrew to her position behind the counter—where she picked up the newspaper and pretended to read it.

Sister Eileen drew Father Rios toward the north wing of the building, to another grand corridor with another imposing set of fire doors, open but available in case of disaster. He did not feel much reassured by their presence.

"Come along, Father. I'll show you what became of the Pattersons."

She drew him toward to a pair of doors that were fastened with a chain. "In here," she said. She took the chain in her hands and unwound it, un-threading it from the handles.

The padre didn't see a lock. Maybe the chain didn't have one, or maybe she'd removed it earlier.

She pushed the doors inward. "I'd warn you to brace yourself for the worst, but I haven't seen the place since two nights ago. I don't know how much progress the Alvarez ladies have made while I wasn't looking, and besides, I have a feeling you've seen more terrible things, somewhere down the line."

"Undoubtedly," he agreed. He joined her with more curiosity than dread.

The hall was enormous—larger even than the lobby. The oversized effect was heightened by the tall ceiling, decorated with an oversized crystal-and-iron chandelier which occupied an astonishing portion of the space above them. Laid out across the room, a series of round tables were large enough to seat eight to ten people apiece, and they were draped with linen tablecloths the color of the ocean. Some tables still featured their silver place settings and folded napkins. Some did not.

The chandelier was not lit, but the last of the weak, milky daylight spilled through the hastily drawn curtains, all eight panels of which ran the length of four tall windows spanning the western wall.

The padre squinted, letting his eyes adjust. Letting them show him more. He needed to look.

He closed his eyes, and opened them again.

At first he saw only the circles: the tables, the chandelier, the round place settings, the bulbous glass lamps on the walls. The splashy blue pattern in the tiles. Circles upon circles. A room that made him feel dizzy, even as he stood still—just inside the doorway.

He let the dizziness take him, only a little.

He looked, and he let the lines blur between now, and before.

Now, he saw dark streaks splashed across the curtains, up and down them in no pattern at all. Before, they had been fresh blood, running in rivulets and cast about in a spray. Before, there had been a man's body, pierced and twisted, wrung-out like laundry and thrown to the floor where it landed so hard it'd left a dent—a shattered place in the tiles. An impression of a corpse, cast with such force that every bone had turned to powder; a man hurled with such intensity that the outline of his shape was as clear as if someone had taken a mold of it.

Now, there was a broken table pushed aside to a corner, and covered with a sheet. The sheet was stained and rumpled, and the table's lines jutted up in unlikely angles. Before, there had been a woman, lifted from the floor...

The padre's eyes found the spot, a place where something had seized her, clutched her, and dragged her screaming across the room—her fingernails splitting as she clawed the ground, leaving small streaks of blood behind her. Her arms breaking against the chair legs as she was flung past them and tried to clasp them, anything to slow herself; her teeth smashing against the wall as she was hurtled headlong into it, and then pushed up—vertically, painting a long path of gore behind her, between two windows like a ghastly bunting.

He looked and he saw the angle of her neck when she hit the ceiling, and he was glad (in some small way) that she felt nothing after that.

When he looked again, harder, he saw pieces of her dress and tangles of her hair snagged in the crystals of the great light above them. Hanging there like so much moss, or so many cobwebs.

He cleared his throat. "Did anyone witness...what became of them? Or merely the aftermath?"

"A boy who worked in the kitchens found them. He was bringing in the soup, and by then, it was all over."

Even though the padre wasn't looking anymore, he saw a slender boy in his teens with dark hair and sun-kissed skin, and eyes like coffee. He saw the boy drop the tureen, his mouth agape but silent. Such was his shock and horror that he could not scream. He could not breathe.

"I don't suppose we could speak with him."

"He fainted, and when he awoke he never said a word. They found his body yesterday. The poor lad threw himself into the ocean." She stepped into the center of the room. She stood beneath the gore-splattered chandelier. "Before the Pattersons, there was Silas Andrews. Before Silas, there was Maria Chavez. Before Maria, there was Mr. Martin and his daughter. And that's only been this month."

The padre stayed where he was, just inside the doors. "God in Heaven...then why would anyone come here?" he wondered aloud.

She shrugged. "Word has gotten out, but not so far and wide. For reasons that elude me, the Jacaranda's danger is nothing but a faint rumor. That said, it's the finest resort on

Cherie Priest

Galveston Island, which is an easy stopping place on the way to the Caribbean. Merchants, travelers, sight-seers. Bankers and financiers. They call this the Wall Street of the South, you know—at least that one neighborhood, down on the Strand. And as for the rest...some of us are drawn here, whether we care to be or not."

"Some of us? You felt called to this place?"

The nun nodded. "At first I thought...well, I thought whatever was here...perhaps it wanted assistance. But now I know," she said, almost to herself. "It doesn't scream for help. It merely *screams*."

5

HAVING FINISHED THEIR INSPECTION OF the dining hall, the padre and the nun were first to arrive in the community room for the evening meal. The next to appear was a lean older woman, who greeted the nun as she approached the table. "So nice to see you again, Sister Eileen."

"And you as well. Father Rios, this is Constance Fields. She's been here since Tuesday."

"It's a pleasure to meet you," she mumbled toward the padre, as she drew up a chair next to the nun. Even while seated, she seemed quite tall—and the narrow fit of her pale yellow dress emphasized the long lines that made up her shape. She was perhaps seventy, with bright blue eyes and hair as gray as a nickel, twisted into a bun atop her head.

He raised an eyebrow. "Three whole days? You must find this place agreeable."

"I'm waiting," she replied—neither confirming nor denying anything. "My husband is returning to Texas, from Barbados."

"Then I trust he has been delayed by the weather."

"As likely as not." She folded a napkin onto her lap, and lifted her eyes when a doe-eyed young man chose the seat next to hers. "William," she said in acknowledgment.

Sister Eileen smiled. "Good afternoon, dear. I hope you've gotten a goodly amount of work done today."

"Yes ma'am," he answered. He was a soft lad, not quite fat but leaning toward heavy—and the roundness of his face made him seem young. A fine gold watch chain peeked out of his pocket in a pretty, glimmering arc. It cost easily more than the rest of his wardrobe, which was (in every stitch) the uniform of a very poor man dressing upward, aspiring toward respectability if not taste. The padre suspected an academic.

"Father Rios," the nun offered, "this is William Brewer. He's a botanist, researching the unique plant life on the island."

"Good to meet you," the young man replied with a wide, if uncertain, smile.

"Likewise, of course." He was pleased to learn that his guess had been close, if not spot-on.

"William joined us last night," Sister Eileen added.

"That's right, I did. This is a beautiful hotel, isn't it?"

"Lovely," Rios agreed. Then it occurred to him to ask, "Sister Eileen, how long have *you* been here?"

"Not quite three weeks," she said crisply, and a coal-haired serving girl with a tray full of glasses paused, closed her eyes, and mouthed a silent prayer in Spanish. If the nun noticed, she said nothing to call attention to it. "I believe that makes me the guest who's been here longest."

"By quite a bit," William added quickly. "And what keeps you here, all this time? I've heard others sometimes complain of drafty rooms and rattling pipes. They gripe that there's too much noise, even if the place *is* full of wonderful technology." He waved a fork toward the ceiling, and the creeping fans that slipped back and forth, slowly circulating the damp air. "There's always something clattering around, day and night."

"I've come here to pray, that is all. This is a good place to pray."

"The gas pipes, the fans, the little machines that pull the dumb-waiters and manage the bells..." Constance muttered. "Making a ruckus at all hours. It's enough to stop a woman's heart."

"Well, *I've* scarcely noticed it," William declared. "This place is a marvel, with all its advancements built right into its bones. I may specialize in living organisms, but I can appreciate the mechanical, too. And what of you, Father? How is your visit, thus far?"

"I'm pleased to say, so far I am quite happy with the accommodations—though I have only been here an hour or so."

Constance glowered down at her plate, as a second serving girl delivered a serving of roasted potatoes and baked chicken. "Give this place another hour," she said. "Maybe two."

"I beg your pardon?"

"Or less than that. It won't take long. It never does." She stabbed a bite of meat onto her fork, and pushed it into her mouth as if she was angry at it.

Though three tables were provided, the remaining guests all gathered together at the same one, for it was the largest. Even the most recent arrivals appeared to sense some unseen peril about the place...even in late afternoon, when the sun would not fully set for another sixty minutes and the sitting area was bright and comfortable. It didn't matter. The Jacaranda still felt cold, empty, and unfriendly; so everyone ate elbow-to-elbow, around a centerpiece made of rich blue blossoms and fresh fruit. They huddled like it was a campfire, and it might keep the wolves at bay.

The remaining six hotel guests included a married couple on their honeymoon by the last name of Anderson; a traveling tool salesman, Frederick Vaughn; two McCoy brothers, passing through on their way to a funeral; and a pretty young schoolteacher called Emily Nowell. They had all arrived earlier that day, and had spent their time thus far exploring the island—and then the hotel grounds before the weather was wild enough to prohibit it. Now that the day was coming to a close and the final meal was served, they all planned to settle in for the night, enjoying the modern conveniences offered by the extraordinary hotel.

Though Constance Fields remained insistently dour, William Brewer stayed insistently cheerful—and while the nun made small talk, the padre observed each of his fellow guests in turn.

He did not have to look very hard to learn most of what he wished to know.

The lovely but cool-natured Mrs. Anderson was not as thrilled with her recent marriage as was Mr. Anderson, who had a great deal of money and a lesser measure of personality. Frederick Vaughn was a very good salesman, and a very quick talker—he and William Brewer struck up an immediate rapport, surprising the padre not in the slightest. David and George McCoy were not so much mourning their dearly departed grandfather, as much as they were wondering about the contents of his will. Emily Nowell was a woman of better means than she presented herself, but an education had given her ideas about securing the vote for women, and other dangerous thoughts that made her suspect to the men in the group—and to Constance Fields, too.

(Though in fairness, Rios would've admitted that the older woman viewed everyone through such an unfavorable lens...not merely young women with unladylike aspirations.)

In addition to the hotel guests, there were three servicewomen—a mother and two of her daughters—who cooked, managed the meals, and cleaned the rooms. When the desk worker Sarah stopped by to collect a cup of coffee, she referred to the mother as "Mrs. Alvarez," and sent the girls on separate errands: one to tend the furnace, one to address the laundry. The oldest daughter, Violetta, was willowy and plain; the younger, Valeria, was shorter and plumper, and prettier as well. The Alvarez women spoke Spanish amongst themselves, but understood plenty of English.

Through the largest window, the padre spied an enormous straw-haired man with a wheel barrow, toting bricks from one place to another in the late-afternoon gloom. "And who is that?" he asked the nun.

"Ah. That is Tim," she said softly. "He keeps the grounds, and performs assorted tasks indoors when needed. He is pleasant and quiet, though feeble-minded, as they say. Sarah has not told me as much, but I believe he's some relation to her—a cousin, or half-brother. She keeps a kindly eye on him, making sure he's housed and fed."

He murmured, "That is good of her," and he looked, listened, and didn't really need to ask—but asked anyway: "And that's everyone, isn't it? There's no one else staying here, or working here?"

"Not directly, no. Others come and go, but mostly stay away as they're able. The postman and other couriers, deliverymen, farmers with produce from the mainland, and a dry-goods clerk who drops off supplies twice per week. Washing powders, flour and sugar, oats, and that sort of thing."

"Where do Sarah and Tim live?"

"Sarah has a room here, or a suite, I should say. As for Tim, I'm not certain...but he doesn't live here. There *is* a groundskeeper's quarter around back, but Tim doesn't sleep there, either. The Alvarez family likewise has a home elsewhere, despite Sarah's repeated offers to give them a set of dedicated rooms. She's on the verge of offering the space for free, I think."

"How would the owners feel about it, if she were to offer room and board to the staff?"

Sister Eileen cocked her head in a little shrug. "I haven't the faintest. The hotel is owned by an investment group. I'm not sure you could point to a single person, and call him the man in charge."

"How strange," the padre mused.

"Maybe, or maybe not. I don't pretend to understand the inner workings of Texas financiers; but most of the Texans I've known are less afraid of ghosts, and more afraid of being penniless," she said with a faint smile. "Therefore someone, somewhere, believes the hotel is profitable—or that it *can* be. The Jacaranda Hotel will stay open until the investors are convinced otherwise."

The padre finished his supper, and lifted his napkin off his lap. He set it beside his plate. "We'll see."

Part Two

The Padre

BY THE TIME THE MEAL had finished, and the last of the plates and cutlery collected, the sky had gone a very dark, ashy purple. It'd be black within another quarter hour, the padre thought as he stared past the curtains—and then stepped out of the way, when Mrs. Alvarez came to close them.

He begged her pardon in Spanish; she gave him a nod that said she didn't really care.

One by one, she drew the long white panels across the tall panes of leaded glass. One by one, the gaslights were illuminated, and they filled the large meeting space with a warm, bright glow accompanied by the ever-present hiss of the fixtures, and the soft, never-ending clanks of the fans on the ceiling.

Mrs. Alvarez went to a control panel and opened it with a key. She adjusted some levers and the fans slowed, then stopped altogether. The night would be cooler, after all—and soon, there'd be no one left to enjoy the faint circulation in the sitting area.

One by one, the guests said their good-nights and left for their rooms.

Footstep by retreating footstep, the place fell quiet.

Then Sister Eileen turned to the padre, and regarded him with those strange gold eyes. "The...the *events*, which happen here—they do not always wait for evening."

"There is no real reason for evil to resign itself to the darkness, though in my experience it often does."

"This hotel is no different. No different at *all*. We should be on our guard. But not here," she added, catching Mrs. Alvarez's eye. "The ladies wish for us to move along, so they can finish their tasks and find their way home. Only those who pay for the privilege care to remain here after the sun has set."

They left for the main lobby, where they found Sarah behind the desk, reading another newspaper, or perhaps the same one as before. She set it aside with a smile, happier by far to have customers than to be alone with the island's daily reports.

The padre looked at the floor, and its sinister swirl of art; he looked at the young woman, ensconced behind the counter as if it were a barricade—as if it could somehow protect her from the thing beneath the floor. It was a sentinel's post, more than a welcome desk.

He avoided the mosaic, stepping around it to the left.

Sister Eileen stepped to her right. Approaching the desk and the girl she asked, "No new missives?"

"Still none, I regret to say." She regretted it enough that the workmanlike smile slipped, and her voice fell a few notes when she added, "I'm starting to worry. I know what you said, but we've been waiting for weeks. I just don't think the Rangers will come."

"They *will*," the nun argued. "But they are few, and the miles are long across Texas. Don't give up on them yet."

Sarah pressed, "But if they *do* come, what would they do? Will they close the hotel, do you think?" The tremble of hope in that last word tugged at the padre's heart.

Sister Eileen said, "The Jacaranda is a dangerous place, and the Rangers could document the goings-on here. They could take the facts to the shareholders, and spread the word to the newspapers, send it across the wires. They could tell the world more easily than we might, anyway—and that's important. Whatever haunts these grounds may not be huntable by the likes of us, or the Rangers either. But we may starve it of its prey."

"We try to spread the word," Sarah whispered. "We try to make it known, but still they come."

"And still you remain," the padre said. It was not quite an accusation.

Sarah looked at Sister Eileen, seeking some kind of permission. The sister nodded, and Sarah asked the padre, "She's told you about the deaths, is that why you're here? Do you think you can help us?"

"I promise to try. So you should not treat me like a guest. You can tell me the truth: Why do you remain, if you know the danger—and if you are so afraid?"

Tears welled up in her eyes, but they did not fall and she did not wipe them away. "Whatever is here, running wouldn't leave it behind. Not even if I went to New York or Africa or China. There's nowhere far enough to run. So I stay. And I serve."

"But what of Tim? Your brother?" he used the nun's best guess.

"Tim is my cousin. He was orphaned as a child and raised by my father, alongside me. Tim..." she glanced toward the windows, as if she could see him out there, working. But here, too, the curtains were closed, and she saw no sign of him or anything else. "Tim is the only one, I think—the only one it doesn't speak to. Maybe he can't hear it."

"An interesting thought," the padre granted. "But you imply the hotel has spoken to you? How?"

She whispered, lest her voice's volume shake the tears loose. "In dreams. The waking kind, when I'm not in bed but I've stared off at nothing, and lost my train of thought. It talks to me in those empty places, when I've nothing to read and no one to talk to."

"What does the hotel sound like?" he asked.

She withdrew a handkerchief from a pocket, and dabbed her eyes in surrender. More tears rose to take the place of those she'd banished. "It sounds like my mother, sometimes. Other times, it sounds like my uncle, or my grandfather. It steals the voices of the dead, if it thinks we'll listen best, that way. But it's worse," she took a deeper breath, and sniffled. "It's always the worst when it sounds like nothing at all, and just shows me what it wants. I'm sorry, I don't know how else to say it, but sometimes it has no sound, no shape of its own. It's not even a ghost, not even some demon out of my father's Holy Bible with the old family tree and my mother's letters from France. It's not even Pastor Williams, not even a creature from a penny dreadful."

"I don't understand," he said quietly.

"That's what I mean. Not understanding, *that's* the worst."

He didn't agree. He'd known plenty of things that were worse in fact, than in theory. But then again, understanding a monster was usually the key to fighting it—and it wouldn't do to argue with the poor girl. She didn't want to fight anything.

She said, "I'm trapped here. Same as Mrs. Alvarez and her daughters. I don't know what it says to them, or how it talks to them, but I know it *does*. They belong here, too. They belong to the hotel, just like me."

"Such despair," he said with sympathy, and as much kindness as he could offer. "It does not suit you. We will solve this yet. There is hope."

"How do you know?"

"Because there is *always* hope. There is hope, and between myself and Sister Eileen, there may be answers. But you must trust us," he told her. "And you must help us. You are in a fine position to observe all the guests, all the mysteries. You must watch, and tell us everything, no matter how awful. You must give us the truth—as much of it as you can. Any detail may prove to be the cornerstone of our defense."

"Any detail," she echoed, swallowing hard. "I'll try. I'll do my best."

"I know you will."

Very fast, almost so fast she surprised him, she seized his hands and gave them a heartfelt squeeze. "Thank you," she said.

"But I haven't done anything."

"You came," she said. "You and Sister Eileen, both. You came, even though you knew..."

He squeezed her hands back, and released them. "We came *because* we knew, and don't forget that. Stay strong, and remember to pray. I've read your King James, and it holds many fine passages for strength. I'm fond of the one Psalm in particular— the twenty-third. Do you know it?"

Her voice quivered. "The valley of the shadow of death."

"There's more to it than that."

"But it's a song, isn't it? Not a prayer."

He shrugged. "Sing to your God...pray to Him. The cadence doesn't matter. The message finds its way to Heaven, all the same."

The padre and the nun wished Sarah good evening, and promised to visit with her again before they turned in for the night—but first, they would watch.

"Before we begin," the padre said, "I should gather some things. If you'll excuse me."

"I understand. I have my own tools—rudimentary as they are, in the face of something like this. But I'd rather not fight empty-handed."

"So long as the Mother holds our hands, they are never empty."

She bowed her head. "You are right, of course."

"I did not mean—"

"I only meant—"

They stopped, and regarded one another with a small measure of uncertainty. The nun's peculiar eyes flickered and flashed, and then were ordinary once again; and the padre thought to himself that this woman may fight empty-handed, from time to time...but he doubted she was ever unarmed.

"I must excuse myself," he tried again. "I will meet you again...here? Or have you some other preference? This appears to be the center, but it's difficult to watch something while standing in the middle of it."

She smiled, and said, "That is an excellent way to put it. Let us meet in the courtyard in half an hour. Is that long enough?"

"Yes, sister. Half an hour, and I'll see you there."

Up in his room, he sat on his bed and removed his hat. Then he removed his black cotton frock, and stood in a pair of canvas trousers and the boots he always wore when he might be called upon to walk, or fight.

He stretched, and yawned. It was only a bit of travel fatigue, but he was annoyed with himself all the same.

He wanted some water.

The hotel had indoor plumbing of the latest and highest standard, with one tap for hot and one tap for cold—a luxury scarcely to be believed. He turned them both to full blast and filled the sink's ceramic bowl with warm, clean water that smelled faintly of metal and salt; he dipped his hands in it, splashed his face, and rubbed at his eyes. When he opened them again, he was staring above the small basin at the gilded mirror mounted on the wall, its silvering bright and new like everything else inside the Jacaranda Hotel (if not what lurked beneath it). The padre splashed his face again, then picked up the small towel that hung beside the mirror. He patted the last droplets from his cheeks while staring into his own reflection.

He would ask Sarah about coffee, when he returned downstairs. He didn't much care for the flavor, but he always appreciated the results.

He checked the mirror again.

Yes, he was tired...but the years were chasing him, so he kept running. They closed in, all the same. Every crinkle around his eyes, each thread of gray at his temples, and all the old scars deepened with every passing season. He was not as strong and broad as he once had been, but he was still strong enough, broad enough. His chest was lean and sinewy, but not yet sunken. His skin was looser at the joints, but it mostly remained a smooth, tea-colored canvas for a dozen tattoos done in ages past—in another lifetime, or it might as well have been.

Not all of the images were expertly applied, and most of them held little meaning.

Some said only that he'd spent too much time in the company of bad men: a scorpion here, a coyote there. A cross on his right inner wrist, done with a needle during his first stay in prison. (It wasn't a sign of devotion; it was a sign that he didn't trust the artist with anything more complex.) A sun with wildly waving rays on his left forearm—the only piece with any color, though it was mostly faded now and the orange scarcely showed at all.

The only tattoo that mattered, was one he couldn't see without a craned neck and a large mirror.

Cherie Priest

It ran across his back, from shoulder to shoulder in blocky, gothic script: his final tattoo. He'd bought it in Juarez, commissioned it by a professional with a steady hand—a man who'd decorated sailors, circus performers, and cowboys alike. The padre had sat down for five hours, leaning forward with his arms wrapped around a dirty horsehair pillow.

Deo, non Fortuna.

By God, not by chance.

IT WASN'T ALWAYS LIKE THIS.

Mexico, 1889
(Six years before Juan Miguel Quintero Rios ever heard of the Jacaranda Hotel.)

West of Texas there were gunslingers—four in particular, banded together by blood and familiarity: brothers Juan Miguel and Roberto, with their cousin Luiz; and a friend they'd known since childhood, Eduardo—a man with a mind unfailingly keen, but judgment unerringly poor. They'd grown up together, orphans in Mexico City. No one cared for them, and they returned the favor in spades.

They took up guns, and then they took whatever they could earn or steal. At first they stole crumbs, and earned mostly wrath. But as they grew taller and bolder—as they had less and less to lose—they stole things of greater value: better food, nicer watches and rings. Horses. Gold, when they could find it. More often silver, for it was easier to come by.

In time, they earned reputations. They earned fear.

They bought better clothes and saddles, and brighter guns with intricate engravings. They went to jail sometimes, and sometimes they escaped. Sometimes they served their time, or bought their way free. One by one, in and out.

The cycle became familiar. It became their lives.

Until one day when Luiz was caught with a rich man's wife, and the rich man shot him dead. Two bullets, one between the eyes, one in the throat. The gunslingers claimed his body and buried him at night, beside a church—when no one could tell them not to. Luiz would've wanted the churchyard for his bed.

"Felon, fiend, and fighter, but still a son of God," he would've vowed. He would've kissed the medallion he wore around his neck and winked at the sky, if it'd been anyone's funeral but his.

They put him in the earth with the saint around his neck, the coin lying flat upon his chest. And their band was down to three.

Four months more, they rode together—when Roberto fell from his horse as they fled a bank they'd freshly robbed. His head split open on a rock. His horse kept running.

Juan Miguel stopped. Eduardo paused, and then kept riding.

Juan Miguel gathered up his brother's brains and bones and hefted him onto his own horse, then rode with him to the small canyon where the men always regrouped when they were scattered by chance. Eduardo was not there, and he never did return.

Roberto lived another two days, his skull leaking through the narrow cot he rested upon, his blood puddling on the floor beneath it. He finally stopped breathing, his eyes still open and staring at the beams across the ceiling.

Later that night, Juan Miguel tried to bury Roberto beside Luiz, but a nun saw him creeping through the churchyard and raised the alarm. She did not raise it loudly. She only summoned the priest who served the small parish at the edge of the city.

The priest was a lean, young man with a serious face and sorrowful eyes, and he caught up to Juan Miguel because the gunslinger would not part with his brother's body—wrapped in a sheet, and growing stiff. It weighed him down, and he'd trudged only halfway back to his horse when the young priest stopped him with a word.

"*Esperar.*"

Exhausted, crippled with grief, and alone in all the world... Juan Miguel hesitated. He shifted his grip on his brother, and he faced the priest with surrender. He had nothing left to fight with.

"Wait," the priest said again. "I will get a shovel. I will help you dig."

When it was done, and when there was a mound of dirt and a makeshift cross above Roberto's mortal remains, the priest said his prayers and Juan Miguel stayed silent.

"Have you anything left?" the priest asked. "Anyone?"

He shook his head, but could not unclench his throat to speak.

A small lantern spit and fizzled from its perch atop a nearby stone. By its light, the priest looked down at his guest's forearm—and he saw the large crucifix which had been so badly applied there. "Do you believe in anything?" he asked. "Anyone?"

Juan Miguel did not know, so he did not speak. He did not move his head.

"There's another way. I think you should consider it."

"It's too late for that," he whispered.

"Better late, than never."

But not there, so close to the city where the four bandits had made their names.

***

Cherie Priest

In time, with patience, and with far greater trust than Juan Miguel deserved by his own admission...the young priest made arrangements elsewhere. There was a new chapel, much closer to Texas—but much farther from the capital—in a place called El Huizache. It was a place to start over, a new life bought with a promise: *never again*.

Juan Miguel Quintero Rios did not make his promise to the priest. He promised higher than that, as high as he could reach: Alone at night, he knelt before the icon of Mary, lit his candles, crossed himself, and he vowed, "Never again. I will never touch the guns again."

He kept them all the same, wrapped in his brother's shirt. Everything a reminder, everything a debt to be paid. Too heavy to carry, too important to leave behind.

The gleam of the handsome six-shooters never dulled, and their delicate whorled designs never grew faint from repeated handling; and when the newly reborn "Juan Rios" arrived to shepherd the men and women of El Huizache, he put the guns inside the altar—atop the relic box.

Within that box rested a tooth and a bone that might have come from a knuckle. Regardless of its precise origin, both pieces had once belonged to a saint named "Macarius" according to the note the new padre was given.

He debated the wisdom of stashing the guns with the relic.

On the one hand, it felt like sacrilege—those guns had threatened, harmed, and even murdered. On the other, they were holy after a fashion. Every day that passed, every hour, every second he left them where they were and did not draw them, did not turn them in his hands, did not run his fingers over the inlaid handles or the rich designs...they were his promise to the Mother.

He chose to believe that She understood.

***

Two years passed.
And then Eduardo returned.

He returned quietly the first time—strolling into the chapel at midday, on a Thursday, when no one was present except for Juan Rios and the lone altar boy who swept the floors and scraped wax off the windowsills. The padre flashed the child a warning look, and he left without finishing.

The two men faced one another in the center aisle, with the cross and the Mother watching them both.

Eduardo stood with his feet apart, hands on his hips. Almost the pose of a man about to draw, but not quite. His hair was longer but his clothes were no cleaner, no better mended. He did not look very different, except for a dark tattoo that snaked out from his collar, and up along his neck.

"What the hell is this?" he asked, waving one hand at the pews, the candles, the padre.

"Things change."

"People don't," he countered, eyeing the chapel and all its modest accouterments. "What game is this? What plan? Are you learning about a new treasure, buried someplace beyond the town?"

"If there's any such treasure, I'm unaware of it."

"It's a shithole, this place."

"It's my home now."

Eduardo lowered his eyebrows, and narrowed his gaze. "I don't believe that. I don't believe any of this. You look ridiculous in that frock. Mother of God, what would Roberto say?"

"Not much. Him or Luiz, either. And if you're going to swear, you could at least do it outside." The padre turned his back. He pretended to tend the candles. He was careful to keep his eyes off the altar.

"There must be *something* of value here."

Juan Rios did not like the tone, or the implication. He'd used it before himself, and he knew it for the threat it was. "There is much of value here. Treasure in Heaven, or a map to take you there." He waved toward the cross, the Mother. "Otherwise, as you said yourself: There's little to recommend the place. No money here, just farmers and cooks, serving girls and the caballeros who come and go with the season. If it's treasure you want, you'll find more of it almost anywhere else."

"Then why are *you* still here?"

"I told you," he sighed, and turned around again.

Eduardo's hand was on his gun, not brandishing it, but resting there—an old stance, an easy pose that Juan Rios remembered very well. He remembered the feel of a gunbelt slung around his pelvis, the weight of the firearms and the calluses they'd rub through his trousers, against his hipbones.

"I don't believe you. You are a liar, same as me."

"There's nothing here for you. You left me once, so leave me again. The first time, it turned out to be a favor. Do it again, and I'll remember you well. If you have any friends, they can bury you here in the yard. That's all I have to offer."

"But people pay tithes. They pay their pennies to the church."

"Not very many. You could find more beside the road, lost by the stagecoach drivers. Search the place if you want, I don't really care. I'm telling you the truth. You should try it sometime. I find it…liberating."

But Eduardo did not search the chapel. He turned on his heel and left.

He did not return until mass, on the following Sunday.
He did not return alone.

Eduardo came back noisily this time, with twelve men at his side.

They burst into the chapel together and fired their pistols into the ceiling, raining adobe and splinters down onto the people who came there to pray and be blessed. They strolled up and down the center aisle, and made sure everyone saw the guns—they pointed them at everyone, darting their aim back and forth, catching every terrified face for a second at a time.

Old women huddled in their shawls; mothers clutched their children. Babies cried, startled by the sudden noise. Men looked wildly between the bandits and the door, and their wives and sons, and at the padre—who stood behind the altar.

Juan Rios held a black-beaded rosary tangled in his fingers. He barely breathed.

"Up," Eduardo directed him, meaning he should raise his hands.

Slowly, to demonstrate that he would not resist, he slipped the rosary around his neck and then lifted his hands, as instructed. "You've made some friends."

"Better friends. Stronger ones."

The padre nodded. So these were friends who had been bought, and could not be kept except with gold. He understood. Even if Eduardo had any lingering loyalties or leftover sentiment about the bad old days...his companions had no such softness about them.

His eyes flickered to Anna Perez, bobbing gently back and forth. Praying. Her hair fallen across her face. She was beautiful, and she did not want these men to see her; she was young, but she understood plenty about how the world worked. In the last row, the Garcia twins—eleven years old, had been sent to pray for their aunt. Both of them radiated panic and a desire to run for the door, but the padre knew they'd never reach it. Down front was the widow Santos, ninety years old. Frail and shaking, wearing a silver locket with a snippet of her husband's hair. She was also wearing a wedding band worth more than anything else in the church, except perhaps Juan Rios's fancy guns.

Which were in the altar.

They were wrapped in his dead brother's shirt, still stained with old, dry blood, lying atop a box that held a tooth and a knuckle bone from a man who may have lived a thousand years ago, and may have died for Christ.

He glanced down at the nook. He masked it by briefly closing his eyes.

No.

The guns were not wrapped in the shirt. They were lying naked, back to back. Handle to handle.

Did he do that? Before the mass? Before the bandits? After Eduardo's visit, when he knew there was a very good chance they'd see one another again?

Maybe then, in a half-dreaming state of habit, he *had* unwrapped the guns and readied them, loaded them. He *had* been the one to lay them out, and prepare them for service. Hadn't he?

Hadn't he?

Yes. No. He couldn't remember.

While the gunmen postured and preened, Rios lifted his gaze and looked from face to horrified face, along the rows of men and women seated on the rough-cut pews. He saw four families with nine children between them; one old man and three old women past the age of eighty; three maidens; half a dozen stray youths, caught in that odd age between boyhood and manhood, girlhood and womanhood.

He watched Eduardo's eyes light up at the quivering, slumpback shape of the widow Santos. He saw one of the bandits use the barrel of his gun to nudge back Anna's hair, in order to see her better.

"Eduardo," the padre said. Not suddenly, but loudly enough to remind his old friend who had been the faster draw, the better shot.

Eduardo took his attention from the widow. "Juan Miguel?"

"Leave, and take your friends with you. I won't ask again."

The friends laughed. Eduardo did not. He met the padre's serious stare blink for blink, while the chaos lifted and rose, conducted like music, by the men with guns. Anna cried out and ducked away, and the widow sobbed, and the antsy feet of the Garcia twins scraped against the floor.

Any moment, it would reach a pitch that meant there was no return, no snuffing of the dynamite's wick.

The padre did not budge. His arms were not tired from being raised up beside his head. They did not twitch or shake, and he breathed as softly, as calmly, as if he were only standing in a garden. This was not his first time. This was not the first promise he would ever break.

Only the biggest.

He'd made up his mind. He only needed one word, one flicker of distraction. The timing would be everything.

Eduardo said, "It's just as well." And with a buck of his elbow he raised his gun.

Faster than that—Juan Rios didn't know how, couldn't remember how it happened—but the padre was holding his own guns. Always the better shot, always the faster marksman... always the first to make a decision, whether the decision was good or bad.

He'd made it now.

This decision. It was probably bad, but not all bad. It *couldn't* be.

In that hair's breadth of a moment, shaved down to an instant so narrow and fine that the padre saw it as static as a painting—as still and unmoving as the icon of the Mother behind him, looking down, watching him break the only important vow he'd ever made.

But this was important, too.

He did not breathe. He counted.

Thirteen men, and only twelve bullets in his guns. Every shot must be perfect, and at least one shot must pull double duty. He must fire quickly—so quickly that surprise remained on his side, for he would not get another hair's breadth to reconsider. Not another bullet, should he miss a single mark.

His mind drew lines between the men in the church, the men only just now realizing that the man in the cassock was armed and prepared to defend the flock. In English, a snippet of the old King James he'd read somewhere, he murmured—"He shall give His angels charge over thee"—while the calculations churned.

He didn't see any angels. He saw targets.

The moment broke, the painting slashed. The imagined photograph torn to shreds by gunfire. Precise gunfire.

Bullets to heads: one, two, three.

Bullets to hearts: four, five, six.

Bullets to backs: seven, eight.

More bullets, more heads: nine, ten, eleven.

Plaster from the statues chipped to powder and rained down on his shoulders. Bullets fired in return, some striking the ceiling, the altar, the icons. The windows. Most of them hit their wayward, harmless marks before the men who fired them hit the ground. Twitching, or not. Each one of them dead before they had any time to wonder what had happened.

It was not even a painting. Not even a photograph.

Two men remained: Eduardo and a thickly mustached man behind him. The other man was ready to run; he'd halfway turned already, statistics or fortune had let him live the longest, and he knew a lost fight when he saw one. Maybe he hadn't wanted to rob a chapel anyway. Maybe he only took the job because he was hungry, or desperate for some other reason.

Well, he was here now. And he was still holding one gun, having dropped the other. Halfway turned, and no—not ready to leave. Reaching for the widow Santos, to hide behind her? To hold her hostage, one big gun to the side of her fragile head?

There were no more moments to split, and only one bullet left in the gun.

Juan Rios hesitated, not long enough for it to matter to anyone but Eduardo and the twelfth gunman. But it mattered to the angles, too…the mentally sketched lines that told the padre where to aim, and how. Two men left, one bullet, and no path that would send it careening through both of them.

And Eduardo, he'd been a friend once, hadn't he?

The answer was "no," of course, and Juan Rios knew that better than anyone, but it cost him the last bullet all the same. He made up his mind, and sent the bullet past Eduardo—nicking his ear and making him swear, but otherwise doing him no harm.

Behind him, the twelfth bandit fell down dead. He toppled over the back of a pew, his backside in the air. Undignified to the last.

Eduardo lifted one hand to his bleeding ear, and looked Juan Rios in the eye.

The bandit did not look over his shoulder to see the shocking state of the small sanctuary. Men, women, and children huddled on the floor, holding their breath, covering their heads. Twelve dead men, felled by twelve shots.

Unheard of. Unlikely. But there it was.

"That was practically a miracle," Eduardo gasped, blood squeezing out from between his fingers. Louder, he said, "People will wonder about it, anyway. The priest with the pistols, killing twelve bandits with twelve shots. They'll drag your name before the Holy Father. In twenty years' time you'll have your own medallions, Juan Miguel."

The guns were empty, but they were heavy in the padre's hands. He did not lower them, though he began to shake. He did not know why. Eduardo, always the showman, continued. "Mark my words, as soon as you're dead these people," he gestured at those cowering behind him, "will descend upon your corpse like buzzards. They will tear your frock, and snip your hair, cut your nails. They'll pick you over, wanting something to show their grandchildren, to prove they were here when it happened. Or, then again, maybe they won't. They may decide it was luck after all. Luck, and the leftover skill of a man who used to kill for a living. For surely, if this were any *true* miracle—true and proper—*I* would be the one out of bullets." He raised the gun, aiming it between the padre's eyes and pulling back the hammer. "It would be me. Not you."

It was only a reflex, Juan Rios supposed—just some leftover memory buried in his muscles that made his trigger finger tighten. He knew the chamber was empty. He knew this was no miracle, that it was only his last breath.

But the trigger slipped back.

And the fancy gun with the silver plate finish and engravings of squash blossoms fired.

Eduardo never had a chance to be surprised. He stood upright, dead as a stone, for a count of five, six, seven seconds; he collapsed knees first, then his hips folded, and he dropped to his side, flopped onto his back, and stared at the crossbeams in the ceiling above without seeing a goddamned thing.

3

HALF AN HOUR LATER, THE padre stood in the courtyard of the Jacaranda Hotel—a wide rectangle surrounded on three sides by the wings of the building itself, and capped on the fourth by a large fountain. He faced this fountain, trying to decide if there was any significance to the patterns of colored tile, or the statue of a woman holding two water vessels; he could scarcely make out any of the finer details, for the sky was a deeper purple than before and the moon struggled to appear, without any success. Only a cool, pale blot marked its place in the heavens, and only a persistent drizzle proved the clouds.

He was reasonably certain he'd seen the exact same statue on a fountain in Mexico City, and the tile was good-quality, but not custom-made.

The nun joined him. She stood silently beside him, likewise staring at the fountain. "Sometimes, it's only art," she said, echoing his unspoken sentiment.

Cherie Priest

A small hint of mischief worked its way into his face and his voice. "If it lacks meaning, I don't know that we should call it art. Perhaps 'decoration,' instead."

"As you like." She took a seat on a nearby bench. He sat on the fountain's edge. It was moist and cold through his frock; the air too wet to dry the tiles, but not yet ready to soak them.

Beside them both, a large gaslamp hissed, sparked, and flared to life—illuminating the courtyard alone at first, and then with the help of five others like it. Now he had a better view of the water fixture, but no better opinion of it; and now he could see the rest of the landscaping: the palms, climbing vines, succulents, and assorted flowers, all placed with as much care and formality as the plates and cutlery upon the supper table, an hour before.

The padre finally spoke again, mostly by virtue of thinking aloud. "What can we say about the men and women who have died here? You told me before that some were called here...were they all? Or were some merely unlucky?"

"That's not the sort of thing that reveals itself in polite mealtime chatter. Believe me, I've tried to bring the subject around—to no avail. But it's funny," she said, her tone suggesting nothing funny at all. "There's such *silence* surrounding what occurs here. Everyone knows, but no one says anything, except in whispers behind closed doors."

"That hardly sounds like the best way to address the problem."

"I know," she murmured. "Or rather, I agree. I do what I can to be open, and to draw others into my confidence. What little success I've met, has mostly been with Sarah—and mostly since you've arrived. You're gentler than me, perhaps. You have a way about you..."

"But so do *you*." He meant it as a polite rebuttal, but he almost understood why her efforts had not been as fruitful as she'd like. It was not merely the habit, not only the accent—so

66

different from what most people heard on the island. It wasn't even the brown eyes, flecked with gold.

Or were they gold eyes, flecked with brown? Everything depended on the light.

She looked up at the place where the moon must be, and he thought maybe she'd heard him thinking again. If she did, she pretended otherwise. "It's kind of you to say so, if charmingly untrue. But would you look up there," she tilted up her chin, to direct his attention. "Not a star to be seen, and getting damper by the hour."

"The storm is almost upon us. Let us pray we're not washed away in our sleep."

"Oh, I don't think it will find us tonight. Maybe tomorrow. In the wee hours, if we aren't particularly lucky."

He nodded, at her and the roiling indigo blanket above, where only a rare, stray twinkle broke through the darkness. "Will the hotel survive it, do you think?"

"It might," she mused. "It's a solid building, made to withstand the coastal storms; but we're quite vulnerable here, you know. The island is long and narrow, and flat as a pan. It's a lovely place, to be sure...but we must be honest with ourselves: It's little more than a sandbar, wallowing between the Gulf and Texas. A better question might be, 'Will *we* survive the storm, should it catch us here?'"

"I am confident of your resourcefulness."

"And I am confident of yours. More than you are, perhaps."

He considered his response, not knowing how much she needed to hear—or how much of the truth she wanted. Finally he said, "We all walk this earth on borrowed time, but mine is borrowed against something greater than death. I do not know what awaits me on the other side, and I do not know when I can expect to arrive there. These *missions*, if that's what they are... one of them will be my last. I am due a reckoning."

"We all receive our reckoning, in time. None of us knows when."

"This is...different," he tried to explain. But Sister Eileen did not ask for clarification, and he gave up trying to offer any.

"I'll take you at your word. But tell me, what do you feel about this place? Use whatever vision or intuition you've been given, and *look*. Try to *listen*. We're not at the center of the hotel anymore. We stand outside it, looking in. From here, what does this place say to you?"

"It says..." he closed his eyes, and opened them again.

He looked, and he listened.

He saw darkness, purple and black, and motionless at a glance.

But no, it moved. It swirled so hugely that it only appeared to hold still—the same illusion of watching a swift-sailing ship in the distance, seeming to creep across the waves. If the darkness had a shape, he could not discern it; but he sensed that it spun in a circle, tendrils dragged along its exterior to flail and wave and cut. A wheel of blackness, revealed only at the edges where it shifted against the earth, and scratched against the clouds.

The padre heard the rushing roar of something larger than the island by a thousand-fold, shouting at the earth and everyone who crawled upon it. Offshore, still. Something that would devour half the ocean, and use it to blast the land clean.

But was he hearing the hotel, or the coming storm?

"It wants to consume," he said quickly, before he'd given himself a chance to think about it. "It exists to feed."

"But is it tethered here, or only drawn here?"

"Both, perhaps. Something tethered and angry, calling to something free but angrier still. The hunger..." he said in a whisper. "I feel its *hunger*—and the certainty that whatever becomes of us, we deserve it—each and every one." He turned the question to her: "But what about you? What does this place tell *you*?"

"It tells me that I'm out of my depth," she said flatly. "Yet I must remain."

A small spatter of rain flicked against the padre's cheek. He wiped it away and waited for a second drop to come, and it did, followed by another. He looked up and saw only the swirling clouds, backlit from second to second by fractured bits of lightning that never hit the earth.

"It's not the storm. Not yet," the nun said. "Merely a promise."

"This place doesn't make promises. It makes threats."

"Then never mind all this. Let's go back inside."

He was not quite surprised by her antsy inclination to return to the hotel.

He did not share that inclination, not in the slightest—he'd just as soon pack his things and leave immediately, and only his sense of duty prevented him...or duty, combined with some fatalistic certainty that it wouldn't matter. He already knew there wasn't time to leave. The storm was too near, and too big to escape from, now; it'd take him one way or another, if the gaping maw beneath the Jacaranda didn't take him first.

Constance Fields stood pale and motionless in the lobby, standing squarely upon the storm-shaped mosaic as if she were pinned there. She faced the front doors. They were open, and though the woman stood unmoving and gazed with hard intent, there was nothing to see outside except for the immense and gusty darkness, staggering past.

She did not speak, and she did not blink while the wind rose and fell, not so strong yet—not really. It did not billow and bluster with enough power to slam those heavy doors, on their oversized hinges. They were oak, each one the size of a dining room table; but still they rattled back and forth.

The hotel's office opened with a creak, and Sarah appeared behind the counter. "Good heavens!" she exclaimed, and she charged toward the swinging, swaying front doors to wrestle them shut. "We can't have that, not with a storm coming in."

"Tomorrow," the nun said softly. "This is only the preamble."

No one but the padre heard her.

When the doors were closed again, and the last of the breeze died down, Sarah turned her attention to the woman in the lobby. "Mrs. Fields, are you all right? Did *you* open those doors? We ought to keep them secured, so the tempest stays out. I hate to lock them," she nattered on in the face of this particular new strangeness. "Other guests might arrive, but I suppose they can always knock if they want to come inside that badly."

Constance Fields relented, and wrenched her eyes away from the doors—to fix them now upon Sarah. "We ought to lock them all, immediately. And the windows too. Keep the whole world out, for its own good…because it's too late for ours."

"Now, Mrs. Fields," she chided. "Come on, and I'll see you back to your room. Are you feeling well? Can I get you anything to drink?"

"No. To all of that."

Sister Eileen lifted her face, and her eyes flashed. Her nostril twitched. She whispered the word, "Blood." Then she stepped forward, out of the rear entrance corridor where she and the padre had lingered. She approached Constance Fields. "You're not all right, are you? No, you're not all right at *all*."

Constance Fields gave a great sniffle, and a trickle of blood slipped out of her nose. It pooled briefly in the divot above her lip, then curled over it, and splashed down the front of her dress.

Sarah's eyes went wide, her pupils as big as coins. She stepped aside, and the nun tried to take Mrs. Fields by the shoulders. When the woman wouldn't be turned, Sister Eileen walked around her, and paused.

She looked over her shoulder at the padre, then again at Mrs. Fields's back. She took a deep breath and said to Sarah, "My dear, I'll need some rags and hot water."

But the steadfast Mrs. Fields said, "Don't trouble yourselves."

Sister Eileen insisted calmly, "You need to sit down. You're bleeding."

"I'm aware."

The padre joined them, and he saw how the rear of her dress was slashed, raked by claws or knives or something else that had cut her deeply. Gouges bubbled with every breath she took, and bits of bone showed through in bright white flecks. Shreds of fabric dangled down to trail the back of her legs, all of it wet and ruined.

"*Señora*," he urged. "Please, come take a seat."

If she felt any pain at all, she did not appear bothered by it. "I do not wish to take a seat. I wish to wait for my husband."

The nun persisted: "Please, lie down. You need medical attention and I...I have a little training. You can't possibly have the strength to stand much longer."

With a rasp at the edge of her voice, she replied, "I have what strength it gives me. I lose what it takes, the same as everyone else." One shoulder drooped, and a dribble of blood ran down the back of her arm, her hand, and off the tip of her longest finger. A puddle formed while they watched. More blood spilled out of Mrs. Fields's nose, and onto her bosom.

Sarah shook her head wildly and retreated, unwilling to touch the woman again—unwilling to touch any of them, or look at them either, if she could help it. Her hands were only just big enough to cover her mouth and her eyes at once. She stumbled back behind the counter, back into the office.

"I can't...oh God, I can't. Not another one, not—"

Whatever else she groaned was lost when she slammed the office door, and sealed when she turned the deadbolt to secure herself within.

The hard line of Mrs. Fields's mouth softened, and upturned into a faint smile. "Worthless child, directing the traffic of the damned. She's not like the rest of us, though."

Cherie Priest

"How's that?" the padre asked. He held out an arm, offering her strength to lean on or merely guidance toward the nearest wicker chaise.

Like all other offers thus far, she refused it. "Sarah wasn't called here, not like we were. She was only too weak to walk on past. Well..." she swayed, but did not fall. "She can stay here if she likes. Or if she thinks she has to." Her eyes stayed transfixed upon the front doors. "Even hell needs its civil servants."

"But we're still quite firmly on earth. Is it some kind of punishment? Some kind of justice, for a sin left unconfessed?" the padre asked, knowing there wasn't much time left. There couldn't be. She couldn't lose so much blood and skin and muscle, and remain upright for long.

"It's something like that."

Sister Eileen had questions, too. "What about the Pattersons? What was their sin?"

"A swindle. An old man with money and trust, but little sense. They took everything, and left him to die alone..."

The nun recoiled, ever so slightly. "Oh God..."

"The Alvarez women had a matriarch once. A different one, I mean. She's dead now, and you can guess...you can always guess. Silas Andrews had raped and murdered. There was a woman, feeble in the mind but gentle as a..." she swayed again. Her knees locked. "I don't know about the rest."

Juan Rios caught her, and felt the press of exposed ribs through his frock. He tried not to notice the pulse of the woman's breath throbbing through the shredded skin...the shivering spasms of muscles meeting air...or the warm dampness that soaked through to his wrist.

He hoisted her up, and with the nun's help, he drew her to the chaise where he placed her on her side.

Sister Eileen grumbled, "I don't suppose Sarah will be helping with the water or the rags after all."

"Don't be so hard on her," the padre urged. "The hotel is hard enough."

But Constance Fields agreed with the nun. "A woman shouldn't...shouldn't run off like that. Not in the face of a little blood."

"It's not so much the blood," he argued softly. He brushed a lock of hair away from her face, and left a smudge of crimson on her cheek. "And this is more than just a little."

Mrs. Fields nodded, and her lips fluttered. "Tell my husband...tell him I had regrets. Tell him that, would you?"

"I will," her companions vowed, their words knitting together as neatly as a verse.

She closed her eyes, opened them again. Exhaled.

And the only sound left was the drip, drip, drip as the blood seeped through the wicker and splashed upon the floor. One thin stream, one bubbled drop after another, until there was volume enough to spread through the grout on the lobby floor— snaking around the tiles in that sinister mosaic, staining the white bits red, and the black bits blacker still.

SISTER EILEEN LOOKED UP AT the ceiling, as if she'd meant to check the sky—but was surprised to find herself indoors. "I need to leave. Immediately. With my regrets, of course. Will you see to her?" She nodded down at the cooling corpse of Constance Fields in the chaise.

He wanted to complain, to ask why both remaining women must flee and leave him to clean up. But instead he said, "Yes, I'll see to her." He didn't believe that Mrs. Fields had been Catholic, but he'd say his prayers out of principle. "Go on, and do what you must."

The nun vanished, as fast as the flicker of gold that sometimes sparked in her eyes. For a moment, the padre wondered if her sudden disappearance hadn't been a trick—or if she hadn't been some small, peculiar specter all along.

But no, he could hear her footsteps, light and fast.

(*Too fast*, he thought. *And too far away already.*)

He rose to his feet, and went to the office door. "Sarah?" He knocked, and he said her name again with his firmest voice. "Sarah, I need your help."

After half a minute's silence, she opened the door. Her eyes were glassy and red with tears, and her nose was pink from having been rubbed with a handkerchief. She whispered, "I'm not strong."

He knew that already, but he didn't say so.

"I don't need strength. I need a sheet or a blanket, and a shovel. Also, some information: Is there any church nearby? Her own, or anyone else's?"

"No sir. Not until you reach the far side of the Strand."

"A garden, then? Perhaps out behind the courtyard? We must put her *some*place, and we'd better do it before the rain begins in earnest—or before the other guests awaken, and wonder what's occurred."

Sarah furrowed her brow. "But what about the police? Should we call them?"

"They must be tired of hearing from you, by now—and whatever occurs here, it occurs outside the Rangers' authority. Besides, they've made it rather clear they aren't coming. We'll see to Mrs. Fields ourselves," he concluded firmly.

"You're right, I know you're right. I don't know why I even suggested it. I should...I should clean this up."

"First, you must help me. There's a groundskeeper's shed, isn't there?"

"Tim's not there," she murmured, her gaze darting restlessly between the body, the mosaic, the doors—which still trembled ever so slightly in their frames. She hugged her own shoulders. "If he was, he'd help you dig. But I can...I can get some sheets. You want me to wrap her up?"

He did his best to remain patient. "Please cover her, at the very least. I can take care of the rest. And never mind the shed," he said under his breath. "I'll find it on my own."

The shed was locked when he finally stumbled upon it, but that did not stop him for long; and it was dark inside, but the lamps in the nearby courtyard cast enough light to show him what he needed. In stark outlines he saw a row of rakes, hoes, and shears; he ran his hands over shelves and found buckets, trowels, burlap bags, pouches of seeds, paint brushes, and other things he couldn't quite identify by touch. And there, in the backmost corner, he found three shovels of varying sizes.

He chose the largest, and while he was at it, he grabbed a hoe with sharp metal tines.

Back inside the lobby, Sarah had found some sheets, a bucket and mop, and a length of rope—and one of these sheets was tucked around Mrs. Fields.

Juan Rios told her she'd done a good job, and while the girl occupied herself with the cleaning supplies, he lifted the corpse and swaddled it—using the rope to secure the wrappings around her waist, feet, and neck. He put her over his shoulder, where she hung as angular and lifeless as a sack of sticks.

Wet sticks, he thought, as dampness seeped through his sleeve, and smeared against his neck.

And he set out to dig a grave.

Behind the fountain, between the shrubbery and the cold-brick wall of the hotel itself...he lifted the sharp-tined hoe and used all his weight to slam it into the ground. Over the years, and over too many graves, he'd learned efficiency.

Don't start with the shovel. Start with the hoe. Better leverage. Easier on the back.

He brought the hoe down again, rocked it back and forth, and lifted forth a chunk of turf the size of a dinner plate.

Rain still came down in fits and starts, speckling his black cassock. But the night air was mild enough that he could remove it, and he did—giving his shoulders and elbows better range to swing, again and again, until there was a long, shallow hole.

And now it was time for the shovel.

Scoop after scoop, alone in the dark, naked from the waist up. He dug until there was enough depth and enough width, that if he folded Mrs. Fields's knees up to her chest, she'd still be eighteen inches deep.

He would've preferred the traditional six feet, but it was dark, and he was tired, and there was still so much work to be done.

If it might have waited until morning, he supposed, he could've imposed upon Tim—he could've let Sarah offer directions, and allowed someone else to handle this part of Mrs. Fields's death. In the morning, he could've given the strange and violent demise of the poor woman a closer examination. The light of day might have told him more than the shadows did.

But in the morning, who knew?

Maybe Sister Eileen was wrong, and the storm would bring its full force to the island sooner than expected. For all he knew, in the morning, everyone and everything might lie in pieces, murdered by the carnivorous hotel—their remains unceremoniously scattered about the lobby.

Maybe none of them would live to see the dawn, and there would be no one left to dig any graves.

He finished his task and returned the tools to the shed, closing it up behind himself. Although he'd removed his frock, he hadn't done so in time to keep it from all of the sweat and mud. It was filthy, and so was everything else—but what could he do about it? He considered the sink in his room, but upon second thought, the hotel must have some sort of formal laundry.

Without too much difficulty, he found it down a corridor on the first floor. Lined against the wall were washing machines the size of wheelbarrows, but he didn't know how to use them; so he was relieved to discover a huge sink of the ordinary variety. Beside the sink sat a bar of soap as big as his shoe.

He rinsed his frock and left it to dry, hanging beside a row of pillowcases clipped upon a line. He hoped it would air out quickly; he felt naked without it. But in the meantime, he borrowed a uniform shirt—something too large, something that might have been Tim's. It was free of blood and mud, and Tim wasn't present to object, so the padre buttoned himself inside it.

Back in the lobby, he found nothing.

No one. Just a large wet spot on the floor, and a chaise with a missing cushion. Sarah had vanished, and so had her pail and mop, and whatever rags she'd used to scrub the place.

"You should see this."

He jumped, and turned around.

"I'm sorry," said Sister Eileen. "I didn't mean to frighten you."

He waved her apology away. "It's fine. I'm glad to see you again," he confessed, and only then realized that he'd been worried for her well-being. In such a place, with such a terrible darkness swirling at its center, he was comforted to see that she was still standing. She made him feel less alone.

"I'm sorry I left you, but I was overwhelmed. Now come with me, if you don't mind. You should see her room. You should see where it happened. You should see what it did."

Constance Fields had been dead a little less than two hours.

In that time, she had been buried and the evidence of her death had been largely erased; and in that time, Sister Eileen had gone to the woman's room and let herself inside. "I found it like this," she said, nodding toward the ceiling, the walls, the bed, the curtains, and every other surface that had been splashed with blood. It was all drying to a brownish crimson, leaving the linens stiff and the floor sticky.

"It's strange," the nun said, and then let out an awkward little laugh. "I mean, it's all strange, obviously—but the front of Constance's dress didn't have a spot of blood upon it—not until her nose began to bleed. All the damage was behind her; she must have turned her back on it, and refused to look. Isn't that...strange? Don't you think?"

"Not in the slightest," the padre replied with a shrug. "If something with that kind of power attacked me, I wouldn't want to see it either. We're speaking of something that kills with creativity and malice, and so far, no one's set eyes on it, and lived to tell. If it seizes a woman from behind, and uses her body to paint a room with blood, or if it grabs a couple and hangs their skin like wallpaper...there's no pattern to it, no rules the dark force follows, as far as I can tell. None apart from strangeness."

"And just like that, the strangeness becomes the ordinary. It's the one thing we can predict."

He agreed, but did not mention it—for his attention was dragged away from their conversation, yanked from detail to detail in the ruined hotel room. A broken bedpost, a long, curved arc of blood spray on the mirror. A steamer trunk half unpacked, its rumpled contents strewn across the floor—where bloody footprints were ground into the rug. "It's a mess, that's all. No message spelled out, no notes left behind."

"But why Constance? What did it want with her?"

"Why *not* Constance?" he countered. "Why not any of us?"

The nun shrugged softly, uncertainly. Then she straightened and said, "Oh dear...what should we tell her husband, when he arrives? *If* he arrives," she amended.

"Should the time come, we will tell him the truth. A gentle version...perhaps she died in some strange accident."

"What if he wants to claim her body, and bring it home to a family plot?"

"We're getting ahead of ourselves," he said, just a hint of crossness in his words. "She's dead, and we don't know why."

"No, we don't," she agreed diplomatically. "And there's a chance we never will. Do you think there's anything to be learned from the room? Any reason we shouldn't have Sarah clean it?"

"It'd be better to do as Constance suggested, and burn the place to the ground." He thought of Sarah, so fragile and nearly useless; he thought of the next guest who might occupy the room. "But leaving that option aside for now, I suggest we lock the door and leave it. There are many other rooms, ready to collect other unhappy souls."

Sister Eileen sighed. "I have no objections to that plan—and I'd be surprised if Sarah did. Besides, it's getting late."

"We're on the far side of late; we've nearly come around again to 'early.' We should rest, while there's still time and peace enough to do so. If the storm comes tomorrow..." he wasn't sure where he meant to take the thought.

"If the storm comes tomorrow," the nun echoed, and the padre saw exhaustion on her face, in the shadow of her habit. "Then we'll all be trapped inside until it's finished. And even should the hotel stand when the worst is over, I don't know if any of us will escape the place alive."

"It's only a storm. We mustn't assume the worst."

Part Three

The Ranger

THE PADRE ATE BREAKFAST ALONE in the oversized hall that presently passed for a dining area. It was early—far earlier than he'd prefer to be awake, given the previous night's adventures, but he'd never been able to sleep very long past dawn. In drips and drabs, the surviving guests came and went, taking coffee and toast, fruit and milk. Some sat down at the large round tables with a newspaper for distraction, and others carried the meals back up to their rooms.

Unlike the evening before, when everyone clustered together, that morning they scarcely spoke to one another—or to Mrs. Alvarez either; and when they moved, they shuffled about like phantoms in a daze. The light made all the difference.

Their calm, passive demeanor belied the scene outside the great hall's windows—where the clouds churned low and slow, as gray as mop water; and the trees leaned and strained, branches whipped out and leaves stripped away with the wind that rose, lifted, lilted, and hummed against the corners of the big brick building.

The storm was coming, yes. Sooner than the absent nun expected, and no one was ready. Or maybe that wasn't right at all. Maybe they all were ready—as ready as they were going to get.

But it didn't feel that way to the padre. It felt like a lie, one they told to themselves and each other: *Nothing is strange, and no one is dead, and no one has anything to be afraid of. The storm will come and go, and leave us all behind. We will all go on with our lives. We will all leave this place, one way or another.*

And so they refused to speak any ill of their surroundings, as if lending the weight of words to the hotel's curse would give it more power.

Or else they knew there was nothing to be done, except look away.

When the padre finished eating, he went to the lobby in search of Sarah. She wasn't present, but one of Mrs. Alvarez's daughters had taken up a post behind the desk. In Spanish, he asked her name because he could not remember it. She told him it was "Violetta."

"Can you tell me, is Sarah all right? She had a late evening, I know. She helped me with a task," he exaggerated.

"Sarah can't be here all day, and all night too. Sometimes I stay at the desk, sometimes my sister does. Between the three of us, there's always someone here."

"Very good. And have you seen Sister Eileen this morning?"

She shook her head. "No, but she rises late. She often appears for lunch, and treats it like her breakfast. Some people are funny like that."

"Indeed," he told her. He might've made more small talk, except that the front doors shuddered, unfastened, and whipped open. The wind almost unmoored them, knocking them back and forth with a violence that left cracks in the plaster.

Outside the sky was sinking, and the water was rising.

But standing on the threshold of the Jacaranda Hotel was an older man, perhaps seventy, with pale gray hair and a salt-and-pepper mustache sweeping from cheek to cheek. He wore a hat and a duster, and when the wind snagged at his clothing it billowed aside, revealing a badge on his belt and a pair of guns.

He seized the doors' handles, stepping inside and drawing them both in his wake. Securely, firmly, and with greater strength than his lanky frame suggested, he wrestled them into their jambs until the wind outside gave up, and let them remain closed.

"Hell of a storm shaping up out there," he muttered. He adjusted his hat, and smoothed his long brown coat.

All around him the room was settling too, the curtains collapsing into their traditional folds, the leaves of the potted plants no longer quivering in the gale. The guest-book's pages ceased their flapping, and the only motion left was the slow, steady churn of the ceiling fans on their chains.

"Hell of a storm indeed," Juan Rios said agreeably.

"I beg your pardon, padre?" He'd retrieved the cassock from the laundry before breakfast. It gave him away.

But Violetta responded before he had a chance. "A hurricane, that's the news from the mainland. At first, they said not to worry; but now the man in Houston sends word that all of us should leave, before we're washed away."

"Yeah, that's what I heard, too," he told her, every vowel radiant with a deep Texas twang. He approached the desk, flashing a polite smile to Violetta and a raised eyebrow to the padre. "But here I am. You got any open rooms?"

Cherie Priest

"Yes sir." The girl flipped through the guest book and found the page she wanted. She handed him a pen, and pulled a ledger out from behind the desk. She asked his name, for their records.

"Horatio Korman," he said. "I'm here looking for—"

"Sister Eileen," Violetta supplied. "I know. She's been asking every day, if there's word from Austin. Every day she asks if they've sent a Ranger yet."

"Is it that obvious?"

The padre smiled with one corner of his mouth. "You may as well carry a sign. But forgive me, please—I am Juan Rios. We have the sister in common, you and I."

"She sent for you, too?"

"That's right."

While the Ranger filled out the provided form, he asked, "And how long have *you* been here?"

"Since yesterday."

He put down the pen and looked up. "Then you barely beat me."

"I'm sure Sister Eileen will join us soon. I'm told she's a late riser," the padre said...but upon saying so, he felt a small flash of dread. The hotel was making him paranoid. "Then again, we should go and knock, and let her know that you've arrived. She's just up the stairs, on the second floor."

Violetta added, "Ask if she'd like some breakfast sent up; I could make her a plate. And Ranger Korman, here's your key. You're in room 221."

The Ranger tipped his hat at her, and adjusted the bag he wore slung across his chest. "Thank you ma'am." He pocketed the key. "And where exactly is the nun?"

"She's in 203, Ranger. Just down the other wing," she informed him with a smile. "Go left for your room, and go right for hers."

"All right. Padre, you go on and see if she's up. I'll drop this off, and join you in a minute."

The padre retraced his earlier steps to room 203, halfway down one hall that curved slightly, even though the exterior of the hotel suggested that it shouldn't. But all the angles were strange inside. All the sharp corners, the straight pathways, rectangular rugs, and oversized fire doors still managed to somehow feel convex to the naked eye.

Now that he'd noticed it, it gave him a headache.

Before he knocked on the door, he listened closely. He heard nothing, but that meant nothing; so he knocked softly and waited. On the bed something stirred, and he was relieved— not that he'd expected anything else, but less than twenty-four hours in the hotel had taught him that anything was possible, especially if it was terrible.

Momentarily, the door opened.

Sister Eileen was fully dressed and behind her, the bed had been made. A small Bible lay there, open to some place in the middle. "Good morning, Father. I see your frock has dried, and you're restored to your ordinary self."

"I retrieved it this morning, good as new—and I'm glad to see I didn't awaken you. When you didn't appear at breakfast, I assumed you'd chosen to sleep, instead."

"I wasn't hungry," she told him. "And all things being equal, I figured the time spent eating might be better devoted to prayer. Heaven knows we could use some guidance, right about now."

"Guidance is good. But a mortal helping hand may also prove useful."

"You've been very useful indeed, so far."

He tried to give her a thankful grin, but it felt hollow. "I appreciate you saying so, but that isn't what I meant. We have a visitor. He just arrived, and—" as he heard the sound of booted footsteps clomping up the stairs—"here he is, now."

The Ranger joined them with a polite touch of his hat toward the nun, who greeted him with an enormous smile. "A Ranger!"

"Yes ma'am. A Ranger who'd apologize for getting you out of bed, but it seems the Father here has beaten me to it."

"Oh, nonsense," she beamed. "I've been up for an hour. Please, let me just close the room—and let's exchange our pleasantries at the sitting area down the hall. I'll ring Violetta for some tea."

"Coffee?" tried the Ranger.

"I'll ask for both."

Violetta came summoned by the bell in Sister Eileen's room, and ten minutes later the girl returned to the sitting area with a tray—then left them alone to acquaint themselves.

The sitting area was comfortably appointed and offered a place for everyone, with a view of a balcony that no one wished to visit. It was barely raining yet, but what drops did fall were hurled against the windows with the force of bullets; and the wind rose and fell, from frantic and wild to uncannily calm, moment to moment, while the sky turned brown, and lilac, and navy blue.

It gave their introductions a sinister backdrop, even as they sipped hot beverages and nibbled at the toast and muffins Violetta had added to the cart. But over coffee and over the sound of the wind outside, the Ranger began to explain himself.

Horatio Korman had not precisely been "sent" to the hotel…so much as he'd seen Sister Eileen's plea for assistance and decided to come on his own. Officially, this was not Ranger business. But unofficially, Austin knew of his whereabouts and was watching at a distance.

"I don't understand," the nun frowned when he told her this.

He leaned into the floral cushioned seat, and stretched his arms to splay them atop its back. "There are only so many men to go around, and you must admit, your request was a mighty strange one. You tell us that nine people have died in the course of a month, through mysterious circumstances and no hint of a killer—at one of the finest hotels in the state. But there's been no mention of it in the papers, save a handful of obituaries, and there have been no complaints against the hotel or its owners."

"Ten people," she corrected him glumly. "There was another last night."

He appeared surprised, but not particularly stunned. "A tenth? But who? I didn't hear anyone nattering about it downstairs in the lobby."

The padre sighed. "No one ever natters. No one ever talks about the deaths, except for poor Sarah...and all she'll do is cry to you about them."

"Sarah?"

"The desk clerk," the nun provided. "Or the manager, perhaps—for she wears many hats. She helped us last night, after poor Mrs. Fields breathed her last."

"Where is she now?"

She looked to the padre. "I don't know...in her quarters? Resting, I assume."

"It was a long night," Juan Rios mumbled around a stifled yawn. "There was a lot to clean up."

"No one told the police? No one summoned the authorities?" the Ranger asked incredulously.

Sister Eileen answered as squarely as she could. "Well, we summoned *you*. In the past, yes, Sarah called for help; and at first, the police *did* come. But after a while...they stopped bothering, unless we asked them to take away a body to dispose of it. It's like there's a spell on the place, you understand?

What gossip finds its way around speaks only of accidents, and unlikely tragedies with ordinary explanations—when any fool could see that's not the case."

"What about last night? Mrs. Fields, I think you called her."

The padre supplied the rest. "It was very late, very bloody, and the storm..." he winced as a tree branch slammed into the window beside him; but the glass did not break, and he did not stop there. "The storm was coming for us. Sister Eileen thought it might hold off, and we would have another day to ask questions...but six hours ago, I had my doubts."

They all kept silent for a long, uncertain moment—watching the gale whip the trees back and forth, throwing flowers and leaves, newspapers, laundry yanked from lines, and everything else that wasn't nailed down...all of it boiling to a cauldron of mayhem, just on the other side of the glass.

"The eye of this thing will overtake us soon, that much is certain," she said quietly. "What you see out there—it's barely a fraction of what the weather will bring us. Have either of you ever encountered a hurricane?"

The Ranger said, "No, but I've heard stories," and the padre shook his head. He'd heard stories too, but none of them reassured him. The stories he'd been told were all about destruction, death, and an uncaring swipe from the hand of God. They were stories of coastlines scrubbed clean by a surge of debris, of entire towns that vanished into the ocean in the span of an hour.

"Stories never tell the half of it, or else they're twice the truth," she told them. "But it's hard to exaggerate a thing like this. I hope that most of the island has evacuated. The official order finally went out before dawn, and anyone who can't leave—or won't—has been urged to seek shelter."

Horatio Korman said, "You should've seen it, as I was coming in yesterday: all the ferries full, coming out of Galveston. I was the only idiot headed *in*."

The padre gave a small, short laugh that sounded like a sigh. "That's how it was for me, too. Now you're stuck here, with us. And with whatever..." he paused.

The Ranger spared him, and summed up quickly: "With whatever's killing people, inside this hotel."

"You believe us? Really, you do?" asked Sister Eileen. Relief was written all over her face, but Juan Rios couldn't imagine *why*. Believing wasn't going to save any of them; she knew it as well as he did.

"I wouldn't have come if I didn't." He pulled out a pouch of tobacco and rolled himself a cigarette while he said the rest of his piece. "Look, I know the Jacaranda Hotel is strange—damn strange, if you'll pardon the language. But I've seen strange things before, and even the weirdest cases have some explanation behind them. It's not always rational, and not always something you can prove...but I've seen patterns, that's what I'm trying to tell you." He paused to lick the rolling paper and tap it shut. "And the way you described it all in your letters to Austin, I got the sense of another pattern. This one looks awful, and I don't know if I can help..." For an instant, his calm concentration flickered—and the padre saw something uncertain behind his eyes. Then it was gone, and the Ranger produced a match. "But here I am, anyway."

Juan Rios let him light the end and suck it until the coal glowed, and then he said, "It's almost like you were called here."

Sister Eileen protested, "No, it's not like that at all. He's a man doing his job, isn't that it? *I* called him here, not the hotel."

"Sure," the Ranger said. But there it was again, that droop to his brow—a thoughtful glance that went sideways, and back again. He wasn't half so sure as the nun pretended to be. "But for starters, let's treat this like it isn't strange."

"How do we do *that*?" the padre asked.

"By asking questions. You two have tried that, I assume?"

The nun nodded. "Yes, but the hotel's guests aren't the most forthcoming bunch."

She then told him what little they'd learned so far, mostly from Sarah. Finally, though she seemed reluctant to confess it, she added Sarah's feeling that everyone was called there for a reason. "But not *you*," she insisted again. "You're not one of the guests, not really."

"If you say so, sister, but we're all in the same boat now—so I'm not sure it matters any, who called whom. Besides that, do you think she meant that folks were called here...or they were *sent* here?" he asked.

"I don't understand..."

He tried again. "Do you think they're lured here by the hotel, or do you think they're sent here by some other power? That's what I'm wondering: What if this is where you go, when it's your turn to go to hell?"

THE RANGER TOOK A FEW more notes while he listened to Sister Eileen and Father Rios; and when everything had been said—everything they could remember, no matter how ridiculous—when it was all laid out, he declared his plan.

"I know you two didn't get very far in your investigation, and I can guess why. You," he pointed at Sister Eileen, "aren't from around here. And neither are *you*," he said to the padre. "But you, Father—you've got a leg up with the Mexicans here...or the ones who used to be Mexican, you know what I mean. What Spanish I know isn't very good, and I'm well aware of how your people tend to view Texians, not that I take it very personal."

"It's just as well that you don't," the padre said.

"With that in mind, I'm an officer of the law—and that gives me both an advantage, and a disadvantage. First, I can run around asking questions and nobody will think twice about it. But second, most of them would rather chat with a preacher than the police."

"We're a veritable triad of difficulties," the nun sighed.

"Nah, don't call it that," he argued. "Let's say instead, that between the three of us...we just might get somewhere. Let's start with that desk woman, Sarah. You think she's up and around, yet? Let's go pester her and see. She talked first, and she might talk the most. Or then again, she may clam right up at the sight of me. We won't know until we give it a shot."

Sister Eileen knew where Sarah's quarters were, so she led them there—to the first floor, where the girl lived in an oversized suite almost big enough to call an apartment. She knocked, quietly the first time, louder the second time, and with true insistence on the third round.

From within, there was no answer—not even a sleepy mumble telling them to come back later.

The nun pressed her ear to the door, very near to the crack; and Juan Rios couldn't quite shake the suspicion that she was sniffing again, trying to catch the scent of whatever waited on the other side. She regarded the two men with an instant of gold in her big brown eyes, a flash of light like a glimmering seam in a boulder. "Something's wrong."

"Truer words were never spoken, ma'am."

"No, something new—something *else*. She's in there, I can sense it," she said vaguely. "But she isn't moving. She isn't breathing. I don't smell any blood, but I don't think she's alive." Before either of her companions could argue with her, or wonder aloud how she knew all that, she declared, "We have to open this door!" She tried the knob, wrestling it back and forth until a loud snap announced that it'd broken in her hands.

The Ranger drew his gun, but the nun told him to, "Put it away—just help me, she's in there alone."

Before the padre had a chance to listen, before he could even come to stand beside her, she shoved her shoulder against the door: once, twice, a third time in very quick succession…each blow sounding heavier than it looked. And before the men could lend her aid, the door collapsed inward with a crash—it banged against the wall and ricocheted, then stopped against her foot as she flung herself inside.

The Ranger and the padre looked wide-eyed at one another, and then at the door. The jamb had been smashed to splinters, and a long fault line had cracked the main panel almost in two.

But there was no time to comment upon the little nun's strength.

Not when Sarah swung from a long cotton belt, fastened around her neck, tied around a heating pipe that ran along the ceiling. Not when her feet dangled over the nightstand from which she'd leaped.

No one moved.

No one thought for a moment that the girl was still alive; no one's neck makes an angle like that, while the neck's owner is alive to remark it. No one soils herself until her body's fluids drip from the tips of her toenails so the rug is a soggy mess, not if they plan to account for it later.

She was wearing a nightdress and nothing else. Not even a bow in her hair.

Juan Rios closed the door behind them, and the Ranger nodded with approval. No one else needed to see this.

"I can't believe it," the nun said, never taking her eyes off the swaying corpse.

Korman could. "From what you've told me, it makes perfect sense. It looks like the poor girl had enough, that's all—and this is the simplest death yet. Or it's the most ordinary one, anyhow, if your descriptions can be believed."

But the padre stood with the nun. "No, I don't believe it either. Say what you will, some measure of courage is needed to fling yourself into the afterlife; and this girl had not one drop of courage to her name. You see, it isn't simple, it isn't..." he came closer to the corpse, and examined it as closely as he dared, at a distance. "It isn't easy to break your neck, not like this. All she did was tie a little slip..." he drew it in the air with his finger, pointing at the spot where it dug in deep against her throat.

Now the Ranger looked too, and now he agreed. "You're right. Hell, I'm not even sure that ribbon, or whatever it is...I don't think it's strong enough to break her. Strangle her, sure— but it'd be one hell of a yank to jerk her neck apart like that."

"We should cut her down," the nun fretted, looking for some handy blade to perform the task. "Are there any scissors, any knives...?" But no one saw any. "I suppose I could climb up and untie it..."

"Don't," the Ranger told her. "Don't, there's no point. She's beyond help."

"She's not beyond *dignity*," Sister Eileen snapped.

"Neither was Constance Fields, but I folded her in two and buried her behind the bushes," Juan Rios said. "I don't know if Sarah did this herself, or if it wasn't her own idea. But whatever has harmed her, it did so without the mess it made of Mrs. Fields. We owe the dark forces a small measure of thanks for that, at least."

She all but snarled at him. "What a disgusting thought."

The wind agreed, chiming in with a fierce whistle that tore around the drains, and hissed through the cracks around the windows.

Korman pleaded, "Ma'am, we don't have time to lay her out. We have another dozen people to speak with, and a hurricane to brace for. I won't pretend there's any chance we'll make it off the island, but there's plenty of hope we can hunker down and get ready for what's coming."

"As if we're any safer inside these walls, then outside them."

"One deadly threat at a time, if you please," he persisted. "One we can prepare for, and one we can't even understand. Let's do what we can for the former, and work on the latter as we go. If the place is still standing tomorrow morning—"

"I *will* bring Sarah down. I *will* lay her out," the nun cut him off. "Whether there's any need or not. She was not a brave girl, but she was a decent one."

"None of us are decent." The padre breathed, "Certainly none of us here, in this hotel, during this storm. We're all of us terrible, if this is what we've come to." He did not finish his dire thoughts out loud, but when he caught the Ranger's eye, he wondered if the old man hadn't heard him anyway.

3

THE RANGER AND THE PADRE left the nun to whatever task she had in mind, with regards to the dead woman hanging from the ceiling in the 2-room suite. Sister Eileen had insisted, and though it seemed pointless to them both, they tacitly agreed that it'd be likewise pointless to argue with her. She'd made a decision. She didn't want their help. She'd join them later.

She'd made it all quite clear.

"Very well," Korman had told her. "We'll track down the ladies who work here, and start with them."

Juan Rios said, "We could begin with Violetta. I expect she's still at the desk."

"A captive audience. Perfect."

Indeed she was there, reading a cheaply printed paperback story about an explorer in the Northwest. She set it aside to speak with them; when she closed it and turned it over, the padre saw a man in a gasmask on the cover.

"Did you find Sarah?"

"We found her," the padre said quickly. "But I'm afraid she won't be joining us. You may need to work a second shift, or find your sister. Sarah isn't well."

Violetta sighed, because his careful wording hadn't fooled her. "You mean the hotel's taken her, too?"

The Ranger cleared his throat, and Juan Rios surrendered. "Yes, señorita. I'm very sorry, but that's the truth."

"I'm...surprised, a little. I thought Sarah would be the last. The Jacaranda needs her. Or it *needed* her. Or...or I thought it did." She shook her head and crossed herself, then leaned forward on the counter as if she needed it for support. "Sarah's been here the longest. She knew the most. She really seemed to understand the hotel, and what it needed. But if she's gone...it surely means the end is very near. If even Sarah is taken, what hope is there for the rest of us?"

Her eyes filled up with tears, and the despair on her face made the padre's heart hurt. It was a familiar grief, and he wondered if it would be his own hell—to bear witness and offer comfort to every doomed girl who served as the Jacaranda's gatekeeper.

What else was he there for? What else could he do?

He took her hand. It was cool to the touch, and faintly damp. Her pulse fluttered at the edge of her wrist. "Tell me, why are *you* still here? You and your family, I mean? Constance Fields suggested that you were caught here, just like her—and like the other guests, perhaps. If we can learn why people come to this place, why they stay, we may solve the mystery yet."

"So what if we do?" she asked. She took her hand away from his, and swiped at her eyes with the back of her sleeve. "Solve it, understand it...it does not matter. It will devour us all, or else the storm will take us." She bobbed her head toward the doors, which shook and hummed against the gusts outside.

"No," the Ranger argued. "No, we aren't going to talk like that. There's time yet, before the storm hits us good—and time before we're all dead, from one thing or another. Now answer the good padre's question, if you please."

"But I don't *know*. Not for certain…"

"Then give me your best guess," Juan Rios pushed. "Tell me why you think you've come here, and maybe you're right, maybe you're wrong. But it will be a place to start."

The younger Alvarez daughter glanced anxiously toward the Ranger, who did his best to look encouraging, but there was only so much his eyebrows could accomplish alone. So he told her, "If there's been some crime committed, by you or your mother, or your sister…I want you to know: I don't care about it. That's not why I'm here. Right now, at this hotel, I'm no officer of the law and I'm on no mission from Austin; I only want to stop whatever darkness is eating the heart of this place. Same as the padre here, and the little nun in Sarah's room."

In Spanish, Juan Rios told her, "Besides, you said it does not matter. If you're right, then what harm does it do to tell us? Unburden yourself. Confess what you will, and you'll see no punishment for it…except whatever we may all find here, at the hands of the storm or at the gates of heaven."

Violetta looked over her shoulder at the hotel's office, then beyond and behind the two men who so gently interrogated her. Seeing no one, she crossed herself again and leaned in close, her eyes red as pennies.

So softly he barely heard her, she replied in her first tongue.

"You mustn't tell my mother, you must promise me that. You can't let her know that I told you." When the padre nodded solemnly in return, she said, "We are here because of this: My mother kept *her* mother in our house, though Grandmother's mind was weak, and she was very difficult. She was easily confused and prone to wandering. She fought us sometimes, when she could not remember who we were, or why we wanted her to eat. She tried to run away from us, but my mother always went after her. She always brought her home, even if she swore at us and struck us with her fists.

"My mother had promised, you see—back when Grandmother was still aware of herself, and when she was first afraid that her mind would leave her. She made my mother promise to keep her safe, when she could not keep herself safe anymore.

"So my mother, my sister and I...we kept her safe for three years, until the night she screamed at my mother and hit her with a pan. My mother screamed back, and told her to *go*—if that's what she wanted to do. So Grandmother went. My sister and I followed after her, but it was dark and Grandmother threw rocks at us. So we gave up and went home."

She lowered her voice even more, until there was scarcely any sound at all—just the soft rush of breath pushed past her lips. "The next day, they found her in the tide. She'd gone to the ocean and drowned. Mother told the police she'd wandered away in the night, when we were all asleep. But we were *not* asleep," she concluded in the very faintest of whispers. If the padre hadn't been watching her lips so closely, he wouldn't have understood her.

He patted her shoulder and asked, "Have you confessed this to your priest?"

"Yes. But it does not feel any different to me. I told God what we did, and I told Him that I am sorry, and that I wish I could have that night back—to do the right thing, this time. Please forgive me, Father, but I do not think that God is listening anymore...not to me. Because when the hotel creaks and moans at night, and the shadows slip back and forth when I'm alone...when the men and women die, one by one or two by two, going to hell like animals into the ark...when I wonder why we remain at the Jacaranda, and try to imagine leaving...I think of my grandmother, throwing rocks in the dark."

Her throat finally closed, and her tears fell, and she would say no more.

To the Ranger, the padre said, "I'll explain what she told me, later." For right that moment, from the corner of his eye, he saw a figure moving outside the far window—struggling to walk upright the wind. "Violetta...over there. Through the window, you see? That's Sarah's cousin Tim, isn't it?"

Violetta nodded. "He should come inside," she squeaked.

"We'll see to him."

"Back into the gale?" asked Korman, even as the padre was stepping toward the doors, and the Ranger came to follow him.

"The man outside, they say he has the mind of a child. We must bring him indoors for his own safety's sake; and though it may be a difficult thing to do, we must tell him what's become of his cousin."

Together they opened the great front doors, and closed them again—using all their weight and strength to see them fastened behind themselves. Then it was only the two men against the weather, the blowing, spinning low clouds that scrubbed the island raw.

Tim was not so far away, only around the first corner.

Even as tall and sturdily built as he was, the wind was hard on him—but he moved against it with determination, carrying something close to his chest and shielding it as best he could.

"Tim!" shouted the padre.

Tim turned to look at him, but seeing no one he recognized, he continued onward—hunched against the coming storm, step by step, alongside the building.

Ranger Korman tried another approach. "Tim, I'm a Texas Ranger and I'm ordering you to stop where you are!" But that didn't work either.

"Tim, please, you need to come inside!"

Their words were whipped around and muddled by the maelstrom, but Tim heard enough to nod, and to call back to them. "I'm *going* inside. You should come too."

"A side entrance?" asked the Ranger.

"Apparently."

"Wish I'd known about it five minutes ago."

"As do I."

Another twenty yards, and yes—they were at the end of the eastern wing. Or was it the north one? Everything was turned around, even the shape of the hotel was distorted, carved, and adjusted by the whims of the sky.

But there was a door, and Tim opened it.

He stepped inside and held it for the Ranger and the padre to join him; and when they were all back within the Jacaranda, he forced it shut with one long arm. (The other arm was still wrapped around something he kept hidden beneath his work jacket.)

"Tim, I am Father Rios, and this is Ranger Korman."

"I know," he said.

"Did Sarah tell you?"

He shook his head. "No."

The padre didn't ask. Instead he tried, "What were you doing out there, in this terrible weather? You should be inside, somewhere safe."

"I'm going to Sarah's room. She's dead now."

From behind them, Sister Eileen said, "For what it's worth, I didn't tell him."

They all turned to look at her. No one had heard her coming up behind them.

She ignored their surprise, and added wearily, "He knocked at her door, and when I answered it, he told me she was dead. He said he had to go get something for her."

"I got it. Can I see her now?"

The nun nodded, despite the uncertain glances cast her way. "You can see her, Tim. I've laid her out, and she's lovely. Come and pay your last respects, and leave your gift beside her."

He opened his jacket to reveal a ragdoll that had been much beloved in some years past. "It was hers," he told them. "She let me keep it, for night time. I don't need it anymore."

Inside Sarah's room, the young woman was no longer dangling—but lying on the bed, dressed in something clean with a very high neck. Her hands were folded across her belly. Tim stared at her, but did not appear particularly grieved. Though that wasn't fair, or so the padre told himself.

Whatever went on in the boy's mind, it stayed there. That was all.

Tim placed the doll beside his cousin's shoulder, leaving it staring at the ceiling from which she'd had hung. It was not a pretty doll, and its face was stitched from black thread—giving it an expression that should not have been very comforting at night; but it was Sarah's again, and that's what mattered to the young man now. He looked satisfied, at least.

The Ranger asked him, "Who told you Sarah died?"

"Jack told me."

The nun frowned. "Jack?"

"Jack always knows. He always tells me."

Juan Rios felt a sinking in his stomach, because Sarah had been wrong. The hotel *did* speak to her cousin, innocent or not. "You mean *Jacaranda*."

Tim nodded. "It talks."

"To you?"

He shrugged, and gave his cousin another long look before turning and walking away. "It just *talks*. It said that Sarah broke her promise. It said she left me alone."

RANGER KORMAN ASKED ALL THE hotel guests the same question, inspired by Violetta's hastily whispered testimony: "When you think of the Jacaranda, and why you've come here, and why you stay here...what memory springs to mind? Was there something you did? Some vow you broke?"

The padre was unsettled by the answers, each of them recorded in the Ranger's small notebook. Horatio Korman's pencil scratched across the paper, testimony after testimony.

A pattern emerged.

But there was always a pattern, wasn't there? When you stepped back far enough, when you were no longer standing at the center? Except this was still the center. This was still the Jacaranda Hotel, and there was still a storm drawing ever-nearer to the island—and soon they'd be at the center of that, too. With every interview, every statement, it felt more and more like standing inside a monster's gaping mouth...ever on the verge of closing.

Cherie Priest

***

Friendly, heavyset William Brewer's face went pale and his eyes grew dark when he spoke of his mentor, Professor Hanson. Together they had discovered some wondrous new species of flower, with seeds that showed immense promise against certain respiratory diseases—as had long been rumored among the Comanche. (Who had surely known of it for a thousand years, and found the "discovery" something of an annoyance, or so the padre was rather certain).

There were papers to be written, studies to be undertaken, seminars to be held...and credit to be assigned. The two men quarreled, but resolved their differences with a formal vow to share and share alike all profits and proceeds that might come of their work.

But. Even so.

At the center of the botanist's confession was a field survey in the Texas panhandle, and a nighttime encounter with a roaming victim of the sap-plague—one of the last to wander undead, to be sure (after all these years). William Brewer could have warned his elderly companion. He might have helped him escape or come to his defense, but when the shambling revenant stumbled upon the professor's tent, the botanist did none of those things. And now the credit and the profit from the flowering thistle (*Cirsium brewsterae*) belonged to William, and now he had come to the Jacaranda.

And every night when the wind scraped its nails against his window, and the floorboards creaked as if he were not lying in bed alone, he thought of Professor Hanson roaming the north Texas wastelands, mindless and hungry, with nothing at all behind his dry and withered eyes to suggest a brilliant scientist, a curious mind, or the co-founder of an astonishing new medicine that might cure consumption.

A chat with the newlywed Andersons revealed a story with a terrible center too—one hinted at by Constance Fields...an accusation breathed with some of her very last words.

Yes, there'd been a nephew—a boy orphaned when his mother died in childbirth, for his father had died in a ridiculous hunting accident, some years before. "Keep him for me," his mother pleaded, as she bled to death in the fine feather bed. "Promise me you'll raise him, and love him, and guard his fortune like it was your own."

Mr. Anderson had done his level best but there was so much money and no, the money and the boy were not his own; and the boy was sickly, and unhappy—difficult enough to like, much less love in a fatherly fashion. But the child enjoyed swimming in the tide, when it came high and close to the Strand. He liked the feeling of the sand and the salt, and on the rare occasions that he smiled, he did so on the beach.

It was Mrs. Anderson, who'd been left in charge... back before she was Mrs. Anderson, when she was only an ambitious governess. She wanted a marriage but not without the money, and there was a child in the way of both these things. A weak one, frail and in need of constant supervision. It was a simple matter to look away. A simple thing, to lose track of him. Easy as pie, finding him floating against the pier, having exhausted himself in the waves. Easy as inheriting a fortune.

Easy as a wedding. Easy as a funeral.

Lean, clever Frederick Vaughn denied any and all knowledge of any curse, any deaths, any unnatural draw, or anything he might have done to find himself at the Jacaranda Hotel—except, perhaps, the idle lure of a holiday at an odd time of year, when the storms were cooking in the Gulf and the heat was often enough to wilt an oak.

Cherie Priest

He stuck to that story until he'd had several drinks, and then several more.

When the bottle was nearly empty, so empty he could see the table through the glass when he looked down inside it for answers, he confessed that there might have been a widow, once.

There might have been a misunderstanding, with regards to her husband's estate. Or perhaps the misunderstanding had more to do with Vaughn himself, and his intention to marry her for the money rather than swindle it away from her. Not that he swindled a damn thing, you understand. But misunderstandings did abound, and she died not long after their union, and his subsequent abandonment. Wrists slit, lying in a bathtub, that's what the newspapers said. Not a tidy way to go, and certainly no fault of the salesman Frederick Vaughn, so his conscience was quite clean and his time at the hotel was entirely voluntary, he wanted the Ranger and the padre to damn well know.

So the Ranger made note of it.

Since Vaughn's arrival, he'd only heard the widow's voice once or twice, or perhaps a handful of times—mostly at night, when the wind rubbed itself shrieking against the windows and the drafty frame let little whispers inside the room. Sometimes, they sounded like her.

Usually, they sounded like her.

Maybe always.

David and George McCoy were two brothers out of three. They were twins, though they looked little alike; and their older brother Matthew was recently deceased, so perhaps it could be said that now they were two brothers out of two.

Matthew's death had been a tragic event, and no one was clear on the specifics. Some kind of accident—there were no untoward suspicions, not cast upon David or George, and that was a fact. No investigation, no concerns on the part of any officials, anywhere.

They wished to stress that point.

At any rate, how could they be blamed, if their grandfather had left his manufacturing company to Matthew? And how was it any fault of theirs, that Matthew was no longer alive to take possession of it?

Thank heavens for David and George, who were ready and willing to assume the responsibility. Thank heavens their grandmother had someone to rely upon, someone to manage the business and the finances. And never mind the gossips who wondered about Matthew, and some weird bargain he'd made with the twins. They declined to specify. The wounds were so fresh, you see. Two deaths in the family, so close together. Such a tragedy, but these things happen every day. Just like the tides, just like the storms.

The Lord giveth, and the Lord taketh away.

And sometimes down in the lobby, they thought they heard familiar footsteps coming up the stairs, just like they did at home. Just like the night that Matthew came home with the knife in his chest, and made it up to the top landing before he fell.

Eleven steps, that's what David said. George said it was twelve.

Last of all, they spoke to the bright, quick-witted Emily Nowell with her pamphlets on suffrage and divorce laws. She wore her hair in an East Coast style, bundled and braided, and pinned beneath a big-brimmed hat that didn't budge when she nodded her head, shook it, or otherwise expressed her shock and dismay at the Ranger's intrusive questions.

Steadfastly she denied any secret sin, any broken vow, or any other reason she simply could not leave the hotel.

She could leave the hotel anytime she liked, thank you very much. In fact, this entire conversation upset her so badly that she'd decided to leave on the very spot, just to show them—and to allay any concerns that she was a criminal, somewhere at the bottom of her heart, in a corner no one knew about. (Or a chamber that no one could prove.)

The Ranger strictly forbade it, given the rising storm, but she stood up and bid him good-day, and added something less ladylike when he protested. There was one last ferry, according to the newspaper schedules. She would retrieve her bags, pay for her room, and depart immediately.

In the end, there was little the Ranger could do to stop her, except to apologize, beg, and warn. She ignored him at every turn. It was either let the woman leave, or hold her there at gunpoint, and as the padre said upon her leaving, "It may not matter. The storm may take her, or the hotel might. It's no better to force her to stay, than forbid her to go."

"But now I feel like it's my fault!"

"No, it's no fault of yours. She was lying, anyway."

"Are you sure?"

The padre nodded. He'd been listening. "Whatever ties her to this place, she can't bring herself to speak of it. Besides, it's no business of ours—and it doesn't matter. The pattern is already clear, for all the good it does us to see it."

And for all the quiet horror it instilled in him, knowing that this might be the last place after all, the last case he ever investigated. This might be the reckoning—and true, anyplace *could* be. Any confrontation with forces dark and treacherous could mean the end of this borrowed time he occupied, and it would be fair.

It was up to the Mother now. He tried to have faith, but he'd tried to have faith in a church, too, and he'd put his trust in a pair of guns instead. His broken vow was a great one—maybe the greatest of all, if you looked at it from just the right angle, in just the right light.

***

A short blast of wind fired a tree branch scraping along a window in the great hall, where soon the Alvarez women would serve up supper to those who remained—and then the place would be secured as best as possible.

The Ranger and the padre discussed it between themselves: There would be boards, and ropes, and shutters to close; they would enlist the help of everyone still standing, and when the hurricane had passed—should any of them survive it, and survive the hotel too—they would bury Sarah, and hope there wasn't any need to retrieve and bury Emily Nowell as well.

But all of that was for later, if later ever came. For now, it was only the Ranger and the padre, and their notes, and the storm outside, rumbling and thrashing against the shore.

5

"WHAT ABOUT YOU?" THE RANGER asked the padre. He still pretended not to see the world spiraling into darkness outside those enormous windows. "Why are you here? The nun called for you, I know, but it's more than that. I bet."

Juan Rios didn't see much point in lying. "I killed thirteen men in a church."

"Bull*shit*, now."

"They were bandits. They came to rob, rape, and murder. I stopped them, and I..." he paused, and let the wind shriek through the hesitation. "I told myself that it was right, but it was not. I did not have faith enough. I took..." he chose an English expression, one he'd come to like. "I took matters into my own hands, when I should have left them in God's."

"But the broken promise...there must be one in your story someplace. Everybody else has one," the Ranger said, glancing down at his notebook.

Cherie Priest

"My promise was to the Mother. I told her I wouldn't touch the guns again. It was part of my oath, when I took my vows."

"But you kept the guns anyway? In the church?"

He sighed and leaned back in the chair, rubbing at his eyes. They were tired, and they were straining. He wished he knew how to turn on the lights, in case it would make a difference. The clouds had taken on a bruise-like hue, and everything had grown dim despite the early hour. "I had my reasons, at the time. And what about *you*? Where's your broken vow? You said that the Rangers did not send you, that you came by your own choice...but that's what everyone thinks. I bet."

"I came because it sounded weird and interesting. This is what I do, I guess—I look into the cases nobody wants to touch, because everybody thinks they're stupid. But I know they're not. I know they're worth investigating, even if there isn't any good answer to be found...it's always worth trying. These last few years, I've looked into ghosts, curses, and angels alike. Hell, I checked up on a chupacabra, once. You ever hear about those things?"

"Once or twice."

"Still not sure if it's real or not, but that rancher outside Oneida didn't have one. He had a coyote with the worst god-damn mange you ever saw in your life. I did the thing a favor, when I shot it. But since you're about to ask me *why*—that is, *why* I've got this interest in the stranger things—the answer is short and sweet: I met a little lady in New Orleans, oh, fifteen years ago now. An old negress, wily as they come, and twice as sharp. She had...power. I don't know what kind, and I don't know who it came from—but she had it. I saw it. And in the end, she used it to save that city."

"She did?"

"This was all back during the occupation, when Texas was there—and when the sap-plague was really getting a foothold this side of the Rockies. Those rotters, they were swarming the river's edge, taking soldiers and sailors, and anyone else they could catch. But Marie Laveau, she understood them. She controlled them. She knew things ordinary mortals shouldn't, but she's gone now." He pulled out his tobacco pouch, and started to roll up a cigarette. His hands shook, and he flinched when another tree branch dragged itself along the glass behind him. "So I guess it's always possible that these days, she knows even more about the world's mysteries than she ever did before."

"And you broke a vow to her?"

He sniffed, and fiddled with the cigarette. "No, not her; I'm sure I wouldn't be here today, if I had. But it was Mrs. Laveau who got me bit by the mystery bug...and besides that, she introduced me to *another* woman..."

"The good kind, or the bad kind?"

"The best kind. Pretty and brilliant. Tough as nails. We were from different places, and different ideas, but we got along anyhow. We worked together, for a while—for as long as I could stay there, and whenever I could make my way back to the delta. Goddamn, but it was never often enough. Say, padre—you ever been to New Orleans?"

"No. But I hear it's beautiful."

"Not half so beautiful as my Josephine. But you want to know what promise I broke, so before you can ask me again, I'll tell you: I promised to marry her. I meant it when I said it, but I got cold feet. I didn't leave her at the altar or anything...I just... *left*. I left by myself, when I was supposed to take her with me. We were going to see Paris, that's what I told her. That's what I'd planned...and I couldn't go through with it. I don't know what the hell was wrong with me.

"Before too long, I realized what a shit I'd been, so I went running back, hat in hand, hoping she'd forgive me. But while I'd been gone, cholera had come calling—and it'd made a mess of the city. Josephine...she wasn't even supposed to be there, when it hit. She was supposed to be in Paris by then." He struck a match and lit the cigarette, then held it like he'd forgotten why he wanted it in the first place.

"Josephine survived rotters and sap-plague, war, submarine fights, spies, and all other manner of things that would fell a lesser lady, and I loved her for it. But in the end, all it took was a batch of bad water to take her away for good." He changed his mind, and took a deep puff. Held it in. Let it out, in a soft white cloud that spun in the air like cotton. "So there it is. That's the worst promise I ever broke. And if *that's* why I'm here, if this is where I meet some...some justice, or whatever... I'm all right with that. I sure as shit have it coming."

For a time they sat in silence while the Ranger smoked and the padre sank deep into thought, and the storm smeared itself across the hotel windows, and walls, and landscaping.

The padre hoped he'd buried Constance Fields deep enough that the inevitable flooding didn't dredge her up. He hoped they would have a chance to bury Sarah, too—and bury her properly, with more than a hedge to mark her passing.

At the thought of Sarah, he likewise thought of Sister Eileen.

He hadn't seen her since Tim had delivered the doll. Had she stayed? Closed up the room, and returned to her own? "What about Sister Eileen?" he asked aloud. "She's been here longer than anyone else, except for Sarah and the Alvarez family. She must have been called here too, drawn by some secret of her own. I wonder what it is."

Ranger Korman asked, "How well do you know her?"

"Barely at all. We exchanged some letters, and then we met for the first time yesterday." He leaned forward, then stood up and pushed his chair beneath the table. "But there's something strange about her. Something different, and I don't know *what*."

The Ranger stood up, too. "Neither do I, but I don't disagree with you—and I've only known her an afternoon." He tucked his cigarette between his lips, and beneath that fluffy white mustache. "Something about her reminds me of the old New Orleans woman, Laveau. Something about the way she carries herself, like she bears more weight than you can see. Do you think she'll tell us about it? If we ask real nice?"

"Maybe. Maybe not."

Mrs. Alvarez joined them, by accident more than design. She rolled a tray into the great hall and stopped herself at the sight of them. "Pardon," she mumbled, and guided the tray around them. In Spanish, she muttered, "The meal will begin in fifteen minutes. Spread the word around, if you like. Today we eat early, so we can get ahead of the storm."

"What'd she say?"

The padre nodded at the woman, and then he said to the Ranger: "Get ready for supper. It's likely to be our last."

Part Four

The Hotel

THE AFTERNOON MEAL WAS HASTY and tense, parceled out in a serve-yourself fashion that required minimal intervention from Mrs. Alvarez or her daughters. There was gumbo in a large tureen, fresh fruit, fried plantains, and corn muffins with butter for anyone who wanted them—though no one had much of an appetite. It was too hard to eat with the giant windows showing off the great chaos that billowed outside; or even after their hostess gave up and closed the curtains. Then the rain began to fall. Rather, it did not fall, so much as it flung itself at the building in droplets as big as marbles, propelled by the heavy wind. The clatter it made upon hitting the glass was worse than the scraping of tree limbs, or the rustling patter of leaves scratching upon it.

The storm would not be ignored. If the guests of the Jacaranda refused to look at it, they would surely hear it anyway.

When it was clear that everyone was finished pretending to eat, Mrs. Alvarez called out, "I need help. The rain has come, and worse will come later. This hotel is our presidio now, and we must make it strong."

"As if it matters," grumbled Frederick Vaughn, who was still drunk from his afternoon of evading the Ranger's questions. If anything, he was drunker now—having finished the bottle of whiskey and perhaps found another to chase it.

"It *matters*," the woman snapped. "The hotel is built strong, but it has cracks. It has weak places, where the storm might find a way inside. It will surely *try*."

Mrs. Anderson sighed hugely, and gestured at the enormous windows. "What do we do about these? Close the curtains, that's all. Hope it keeps out the worst of the glass and debris, when the things begin to shatter."

"Yes, we close the curtains, and we close the doors behind ourselves, and we fasten them." Mrs. Alvarez folded her arms. "We will lock ourselves as deep inside as we can. We close off all the side doors, and block them with heavy furniture. We shut every window, every door, in every room—and bolt them up tight. Then we close the fire doors, to shut down the hallways."

"And the front doors?" asked the Ranger. "They're big and heavy, but..."

"There is a brace for them, a beam. I will need help to move it, but it will hold. Come now, we must work together—before the last of the light has left us."

The padre rose from his chair. "Let us divide into groups, and secure the wings floor by floor. I'll begin with the first floor's east wing," he declared, meaning the place where Sarah was still laid out, still broken-necked with a ragdoll lying on the bed beside her. "Ranger, perhaps you can take the third floor, of the same wing." For that was where Constance Fields had died, and the room was closed without being secured. They'd discussed her death already; the Ranger knew what to expect, should he peek inside her quarters.

The remaining guests chose their stations and departed, leaving their plates and cutlery on the tables without a second thought. Mrs. Alvarez left them too, pausing only to tie the curtains shut at each great window. She looked back and forth between the tables and the chairs, as if she considered how useful they might be…but she discarded any thoughts of securing the space any further.

She threw her hands up in surrender, and when she saw the padre watching her, she told him in Spanish, "The glass will break and the room will be in ruins. We can't save the whole building, and we shouldn't fool ourselves about it; damage will occur, by the will of God. But we should preserve what we can. Sacrifice the one room to save the one wing. Come with me, we should close this door, and forget this room—it is already lost. Let the storm come inside and clean it out, I don't care and neither does the Jacaranda."

He joined her in drawing the big double doors shut in their wake, and then he asked about sheets of wood, and nails. "We can cover some of the small windows, like the ones in these doors—and the front doors. We can keep the glass from blowing around inside, should it break."

"You can find those things out in the shed," she said, then withdrew the statement as ridiculous, almost immediately. "But you should not attempt it. No one should leave anymore, this must be our fortress now."

"I agree, but what about—"

With a snap of her fingers, she cut him off. "Wait—there are scraps by the back entrance. Tim was building a covered porch. We brought the wood and the tools inside this morning, and stacked them in the laundry room."

"Thank you. That is most helpful."

He excused himself with a small bow, and checked the laundry room. He remembered it well, and yes, now there were piles of scrap and tools tossed into the mix of machines, sinks, and lines. He rifled through the building materials and, finding promising pieces and a heavy hammer, he went to the lobby to begin with the main doors.

They were solid as stone, except for those small decorative windows—and through the colored bits of glass he saw terrible motion outside, drawn in hasty strokes that suggested violence and mayhem without any details. He shuddered and held up a scrap of wood, then drove nails through either end, on each side of the glass. Four more such scraps were enough to cover both panes, though he lingered over the last few inches, hesitating before covering the last small gap.

It was only a sliver, and not even a sliver of light; between the hour and the clouds it might as well have been midnight beyond the little windows...but it felt very final, and very futile.

It felt like he was walling up a tomb, with himself and everyone else inside.

He pounded the last two nails in deep, and he told himself to have faith—because there was no one else to remind him.

The nun might've reminded him, but she was absent. She hadn't joined them for supper, and she wasn't in Sarah's room when the padre went to check on the pair of them. He heard nothing inside, even when he listened for all he was worth, and the door had been locked firmly enough that he didn't care to try it. Sister Eileen was somewhere else, then, and no one would stumble upon Sarah's body. It seemed like insufficient preparation, but it would have to be enough.

He stood still and listened hard.

All around him, the cavernous hotel rattled and pattered with the rushing thuds of feet, running from room to room, door to door. Windows were tested, and curtains were drawn; mattresses were lifted and pressed against them, in case the weight would preserve the room somehow.

A silly effort, yes, but all of these efforts were silly. The hotel would stand, or it would not. A mattress here, a pair of curtains there, the occasional boarded-up portal...in the end, none of it would matter if the storm wanted badly enough to find its way inside.

But the fire doors. They might stand sentinel, a last line of defense.

He regarded the door at the end of the first floor's east wing: a massive contraption of metal and wood too heavy to be moved by the hands of any lone man...or even the hands of several men. Thus there was a handle on a crank, and using the simple mechanics of a wheel the thing could be drawn and positioned, and locked with an enormous seal that spiraled and clicked... and then would not be moved without the help of a release lever.

These doors were essentially air tight, designed to protect the premises in case of an inferno. Should a fire begin in one room, and spread to others, the wing could be closed off and left to burn. The rest of the hotel ought to be salvageable. Or that was the idea.

Maybe it would work against water, just as well.

Under his breath, the padre mumbled, "If it doesn't, we really *are* sealing our own tomb."

He was surprised to hear a response, faint and very nearby.

At least you'll have one.

Confused and a little alarmed—had he shut someone into the wing? He would've sworn it was empty—he whirled around, saw no one, and then leaned his ear against the fire door. He heard nothing on the other side.

Then he understood.

He closed his eyes. Exhaled. Opened them again, and *looked*.

Ah, there she was. More solid than ghosts tended to be, in his experience. She might have been standing before him, flesh and blood and a sour expression. He might have reached out to touch her, but he did not. He only stared at Constance Fields, or what was left of her memory.

She wore the same dress, clean in the front except for the blood that came from her nose, dripping even now—in whatever weird afterlife had snared her. She looked calm and bored, and when the padre asked, "Why are you still here?" she shrugged.

Couldn't leave before, and I still can't.

"Why were you here in the first place?" he asked, on the off chance that it mattered. "What shall we tell your husband?"

She ignored the first question, or maybe she didn't. *My husband's been dead for years.*

"He has? Is…is he here?"

She didn't answer that, either. *Maybe the storm will wash us all away. Maybe it will clean this place from the face of the earth, and us with it.*

"You're thinking of fire. That's how you cleanse a place of evil, with smoke and flame, not a flood." He'd done it before, sometimes ceremonially—with incense and ash, or sage and an eagle's wing to smudge the fumes into every corner. Sometimes he'd done it more literally with a torch, and left nothing standing.

This place won't burn.

She turned away from him, pivoting like she stood on a wheel. Her feet never moved, they only hovered half an inch above the floor, and she only glided slowly away. Her back was the same horror it'd been when last the padre had seen her, and her spine gleamed white in places where there should have been skin or muscle.

Even if it weren't for the storm, there's no flame hot enough, she said. *I always thought hell was hot and dry. But hell is hot and wet, and we who remain here forever gasp, but never drown.*

2

WHEN THE HOTEL WAS READY, or as near to ready as possible, they regrouped in the main lobby: the Ranger, the padre, Mrs. Alvarez with her daughters Valeria and Violetta, Frederick Vaughn, William Brewer, the Andersons, the McCoy brothers George and David, and Sister Eileen—who'd reappeared after whatever personal errand she'd disappeared to perform.

The hotel had been searched, and there was no one else inside to gather.

The rain fell in earnest then, drops now as big as plums battering the building like so many fists. The sound was not quite deafening, not quite so loud that it could not be spoken over, but it was ever-present and frightful all the same. It was impossible not to hear it. It never faded into the background, but clamored every moment for every ounce of everyone's attention.

Cherie Priest

Now twelve people stood in the sizzling gaslights, below the dull spinning of the ceiling fans on their infinite loop, the rattle of their chains no longer audible. The lobby was all black shadows and white-orange glow, cast too sharply now that the windows were covered and there was no more sky showing through—not anyplace, even the little leaded windows on the big front doors, with nothing on the other side but storm and night.

The men and women inside couldn't even see the lightning now—they couldn't count on the intermittent flashes to give them a second's extra glow between the rumbles of thunder. They pealed with the sound of boulders, tumbling down a mountain.

Mrs. Anderson couldn't bear the water, the rocks, and the rest of the silence, so she nervously told herself the same fairy tale they all recited, when they weren't too busy praying. "The hotel will stand," she declared. "Of course it will. It's the strongest thing on the island, I'm sure."

"I don't know about that," Sister Eileen countered. "There's a convent a few miles from here, built of stone from the ground up. If anything remains when the storm is passed, it'll be *that*."

"I don't know," said the Ranger. "There's a prison here, built to keep people inside at all cost. Walls thicker than these, and fewer windows. It's a proper fort, and if anything's left when the rain has finished, that's my guess. That's where I'd put my money."

The padre listened to them argue, but then he listened to the rest of the room, in case of ghosts who wished to be heard. He was rewarded by a soft, garbled sigh—coming from the space between the great staircases, where the twisting mosaic of colored tiles darkened a wide spot on the floor.

It will not be the rain. It will not be the wind.

He did not see anyone or anything speaking. He did not think anyone else could hear it, either.

It will be the ocean, that takes you all.

"Who said that?" he asked in a whisper. No one responded, except for the Ranger—who gave him a strange look.

He still didn't see anything. Or did he? Was he looking for the wrong things?

He closed his eyes again, exhaled every trace of air. Opened his eyes.

Yes.

Something flickered around the edges of the room, something dark and unfriendly, but unfocused. He tried his mantra again, and combined it with a small prayer—he only asked for clarity—and this time when he opened his eyes, the vision was clearer indeed: a throbbing set of shadows, cluttering the corners like cobwebs or tumbleweeds...each tendril too thin and brittle to measure, but collected together the bits and pieces showed themselves a shape...a puddle, no—more like a snow-drift that shifted and slithered. Not one thing, but many things that gathered up to make a whole.

All of it dribbled in weird, trailing, tumbling rivulets toward the center of the hotel where the pattern on the floor was not just a circle, not just a spiral, but a thing that *moved* when he looked away.

His breath caught in his throat; his eyelids flickered, trying to chase the image out of his head. It worked, more or less. The sinister shadows and their edges, being drawn down that inexorable drain...they faded back into the corners to mix with the ordinary shadows, cast by the ordinary lamplight.

Never before had the padre wished so badly to see the sun.

"We aren't safe here!" cried William Brewer, his plump, pink face flushing fever-hot.

Sister Eileen did not much comfort him, when she said, "We aren't safe anywhere, my dear. There's a hurricane outside, and there's no pretending otherwise. It's a bad one, a huge one—with wind that could drive a pencil through your skull, if it caught you just right."

David McCoy dropped himself onto one of the couches that populated the public space. "That's awfully *specific*."

"I've seen these things before; I've even lived through them, once or twice. Storms like this, and worse ones besides."

"Worse ones?" Mrs. Anderson broached, almost hopefully. "You've survived worse?"

"Yes, and so can anyone, if you're smart." She climbed up on top of a small coffee table—in order to give herself some height. She was a small woman, for all her unexpected strength; but the storm was loud and the crowd was uncertain and muttering. "Listen to me, we've been as smart as we can. We've sealed up the hotel, we've covered up the windows—and closed up spaces where the windows can't be covered. We've checked all the rooms, and gathered together in the center. The center is…" she faltered, but finished the thought anyway. "It's always safest in the center."

She was wrong, just this once.

The padre knew it, and maybe the Ranger knew it too—but the Texan kept his mouth shut when Juan Rios added his lie to the nun's. "She's right, and you all know it. If one room should fall, then the center will hold. If one wing should be pulled down by the wind, then the center will stand its ground. If the roof above us is torn free by the rain, then the floors above us will still remain. We *must* stay together, and watch out for one another. The fire doors are closed, anyway," he concluded. "We are secure, and we will stay that way."

Frederick Vaughn had a bottle in hand. The padre wasn't sure where it'd come from, but he would've liked a drink himself—and he almost said so, but Vaughn griped, "What if we don't? What if the walls blow down, and *then* what?"

"Then..." the nun threw her hands up, exasperated. "Then we all wash out to sea, and that's the last anyone will ever hear from us. But it won't come to that."

It will not be the wind. It will not be the rain.

That whisper again, that menacing voice that came from the dark place on the floor—the dark place that moved, that gyred ever so slightly when the padre's eyes were elsewhere. "I know," he breathed. "You already told me."

He might have said more, and there might have been more arguing, but then there was a crack—a pop, and a loud crash that came from somewhere at the far end of the northern wing.

The lights sputtered, and went out.

Up above, the ceiling fans ground to a stop.

Outside, there was nothing but the rain, louder than an orchestra.

Valeria started to cry—or it might have been Violetta, as the sisters sounded much alike. It was purely, perfectly dark, and the padre knew where the girls had been standing, and that the soft weeping he heard came from their direction, surely from one of them—over by the reception desk.

"Everyone stay calm!" shouted the Ranger.

"I can do something..." It was Violetta, so yes, her sister was the one crying. "Please, let me pass," she urged as she struggled through the press of frightened people. "Please, move—let me feel my way...there are candles in the office."

"I have some matches, sweetheart," Korman told her.

"Save them. I don't need them, yet. There are some in the manager's drawer."

He struck one anyway, and for a brilliant white flare of a moment, there was light around his face. He held it aloft, and it showed a little more. But only a little. Only more frightened faces, outlined against the blackness of the hotel lobby.

Violetta tripped over something or someone, scrambled on the floor, and kept moving. The padre tracked her with his ears, wishing he could hear her movements better over the rain, and wishing he could be helpful, but he didn't know what to do—and the girl knew her way around better than he did.

The match went out, and the Ranger struck another one.

The padre counted four faces, five faces, six. All eyes wide, every pupil as large as the face on a watch. There were twelve men and women, all together. Wasn't that right? Twelve in all, now that Emily Nowell was gone.

Heaven seemed to like that number. Maybe hell did, too.

The girl's hands slapped against the front of the counter; she drew herself up it, then along it, then behind it. "I'm almost there," she relayed.

The match went out.

The Ranger withdrew another one, but the padre told him, "Don't. She's right, you should save them. We may need them tonight."

"We have a few back here at least, but we can always use more! Keep them, do not waste them!" Violetta agreed.

The padre followed the sound of her voice, and let it lead him to the counter in her wake. He followed her voice, because it made him feel like he knew where he was, despite the blackout. She was at the counter. She was behind the counter. She was entering the office on the far side of it.

So when he trailed behind her, he could believe that he was far from the spiral mosaic on the floor, as far as he could get—even though it wasn't true, and he was still well within its reach. It might have been some irrational, human instinct, the idea that he could scale the counter and escape the floor—maybe escape its carnivorous design. If he could get up higher, remove his feet from the tiles and the designs, it might not be able to touch him.

It was a stupid notion, but still he clung to the counter's edge, and took some slight reassurance from the cool marble top so hard and unyielding beneath his fingers. But he did not climb atop it.

Violetta reached the office door, and found it locked. She swore in Spanish, something about her mother and the keys, but with a few shoves of her shoulder and one solid kick, she'd knocked the knob free and let herself inside. It was only a little crash, when the door snapped back and beat itself against the office wall. It was barely a thing worth mentioning, in that hall where the rain and the rumbling sky were the only constants, and the wind came and went, screaming obscenities.

A minute or two of fumbling—the padre could hear it, between the rise and fall of the weather—and Violetta emerged, bringing a lit candle. She also brought four others unlit, gathered up in her free hand. "This was all I could find," she said with a note of apology. "But it's better than nothing."

"Very good, thank you," the padre told her. "We should've done this at the start, but I guess we ran out of time, didn't we?"

She handed one to him, and he held it still while she shared her fluttering spark. Then he passed it off to the Ranger, and eventually all five candles burned brightly, spread throughout the lobby so that there was light enough to see by—even if there wasn't much to see.

One by one, and sometimes two by two, the men and women chose seats around the lobby, as near to any given candle as possible. The padre, the nun, and the Ranger shared a candle with Violetta—who remained behind the counter with the inertia of duty.

She rubbed her hands together like they were cold, and paced back and forth along the counter's length, never quite leaving the edge. She let the tether of the candle keep her there with them, and sometimes she prayed quietly in Spanish. Sometimes she only stared from corner to corner, from candle to candle, and back to the spiral design on the floor.

Finally she looked up at the padre, meeting his eyes directly. She blurted out, quietly enough to sound like a private request: "Tell me, Father—does it talk to you?"

"I beg your pardon?"

"The hole in the floor, in the tiles, you know what I mean. It's supposed to be a design, like a whirlpool...but it's not. It's a mouth, and the devil uses it to speak from below." She withdrew then, the look on her face implying she wished she could take her question back. "Sometimes...when it thinks I'm not watching... sometimes I think it moves. Does *that* sound crazy, too?"

He shook his head. "Not at all."

"And it's no trick of the light, either," she added.

"No, no trick of the light."

The nun and the Ranger both glared toward the dark spot on the floor as if they dared it to budge, but Violetta told them, "It only shifts when you're not paying attention. I only noticed it after a week or two, after taking these jobs at the counter, and standing here with the books—staring at it, and looking away. The shape changes, like it's...like it's...*spinning*. Like when you pull the plug of a drain," she added brightly, not because it was a lovely image, but because she'd found the perfect comparison. "The way the water goes, as it falls down the hole in the middle. That's what it does, very slowly."

"When no one is looking," the padre added, agreeing with her in every way. And now, of course, he could neither look at the pattern nor look away from it—he could only watch, and not watch, and pretend that it wasn't true.

Knowing it was true—and that whatever it was, it was hungry, and it had a voice.

3

HOURS PASSED IN THE LOBBY and very little was said, very little was done.

From time to time, someone would borrow a candle to visit the water closet; once in a while, a window would crack somewhere off in the hotel's distant corners, and a new shriek of wind would let itself inside, cutting itself on the glass and feeling around for some deeper entrance.

Every place where one small thing broke, the wind and the water got a greater foothold, and they picked, poked, and prodded at all the other seams in case there was more ground to be gained.

Once a broken window, then a broken door—banging back and forth against its shattered jamb, at the end of one wing on one floor. Then another door, and another window, the structural integrity failing a tiny piece at a time, one floor, one wing at a time. The rain prying open cracks, forcing itself between bricks, loosening stones and yanking at the drain-pipes.

Cherie Priest

One brick here, knocked from one corner and thrown into the maelstrom…two bricks behind it, and part of the east wing's overhang—gone. Shutters ripped from their hinges, joining the clattering percussion of things half-affixed, and flailing, and slamming themselves against the hotel until they broke and blew away.

But the fire doors held.

The center held, and the men and women in the lobby held their breath with every new half-heard strike of lightning, and every rushing, train-like roar as the storm surge pushed past them—tearing up trees, scooping up fences, sloughing away roads. Swiping it all across the island, and into the ocean.

But for three hours the hotel held its ground.

Someone produced a pack of cards, and a game broke out between the McCoy brothers and Mr. Anderson. Frederick Vaughn was invited to join, but he only swigged from his bottle and declined to share or participate. Mrs. Alvarez comforted her daughter Valeria, though Violetta remained at her post—taking some strange peace from the position.

She, at least, was right where she was supposed to be.

"The hotel will stand," Mrs. Anderson kept telling herself.

And the nun replied, with a friendly hand on her shoulder, "It will stand, yes. It doesn't have to hold forever—just through the storm. It'll pass over us before morning, or that'll be the worst of it, I'm sure."

"We only have to survive the night," agreed Mr. Anderson. "And we can be on our way tomorrow. We can leave this miserable place behind, once the sun rises."

A round of agreement rose and fell, for now it was accepted that whatever spell had kept them there, it was surely broken by the hurricane—and no one wanted anything more than to run away, and never look back.

Around eleven at night, according to the Ranger's watch, the rain abruptly lessened and the thunder withdrew. The wind ceased its screaming and settled down to a moan, then a hum.

Then a breeze, barely enough to ruffle a curtain.

"It's...it's *done*. We did it...we weathered the goddamn storm!" cried Frederick Vaughn, setting his bottle aside. He didn't need it anymore. It was empty, and he was only holding it like a child holds a doll.

But the nun warned him, "Patience, Mr. Vaughn. This isn't the end—not yet."

"But it's stopped! Look, listen—all of you: no more rain, no more wind..."

"*Patience*," she commanded. "At the center of these storms there is always an eye—a quiet place in the middle, but it will not last. The rest of the squall awaits on the other side. This is only a temporary respite."

"Listen to the woman," the Ranger urged, but Frederick did not sit down.

He stumbled, nearly knocked over a candle, and rallied himself to a standing position. "This is horseshit. It's finished, and I'm leaving."

The padre tried, "No, you can't. Give it another hour and see if she's right. We've lasted this long, another hour won't be the end of us."

"Speak for yourself. I can't stand it in here, not another minute." He rubbed at his eyes, and wiped his nose on the back of his shirt-sleeve. "I can't do this anymore. Hell, I'm out of whiskey."

"What if I got you some more?" Mrs. Alvarez asked. "There's a bar, in the dining hall. I have the keys, and I can give you another bottle. Just stay here," she begged him. "The sister is right, and I've been in storms like these. We're not finished. We're only halfway through, and we mustn't open the hotel, not yet."

Cherie Priest

He wavered, frowning around the room, glancing toward the dining hall—which had been locked since shortly after his arrival.

The padre looked at the main doors, with their oversized beam bracing them shut from within; and he looked at Frederick Vaughn, surely too weak to do much more than complain. Then he said to Mrs. Alvarez, "That's a good idea. Bring in some spirits, and we can share. It will calm our nerves, and give us all a little distraction."

He thought that Valeria and Mrs. Anderson in particular could use the distraction, but if Vaughn would drink enough to floor himself, that was fine too. A glass in moderation for everyone else, and then they would wait for the rest of the storm with a greater sense of calm, or at least a dulled sense of care.

Mrs. Alvarez took a set of keys from a pocket in her skirt. "Padre, could you bring a candle? I'll push the cart out, if you'll mind the light, and the door." She knew he was aware of what waited behind that door, and she didn't care for anyone else to see it. Maybe the darkness would hide the carnage, and maybe not—but it was best to keep it out of view, regardless. The mood was tense enough without any reminder that the hotel was every bit as bad as the weather outside it.

"Of course," he said, and when Violetta protested at the thought of losing her light, Sister Eileen said, "Take ours. It's half gone by now, but so is everyone else's."

Mrs. Alvarez thanked her, and said, "There might be more candles in the buffets. I'll look."

Juan Rios led the way with his thick stub of wax, now barely as long as his index finger. He hoped there was more to be found in the dining area, and he wished they'd thought to collect more before they'd secured themselves in the central portion of the hotel, but there was nothing to be done about it now. Either they'd find more, or they'd find darkness.

Either way, dawn would find them in a few hours.

144

With one eye on the lobby, Mrs. Alvarez unlocked the dining hall and ushered the padre inside it. Their candle was only bright enough to give them a small bubble of vision...and it was blessedly too dim to show any of the blood stains left on the curtains, on the floors, or anywhere else.

All the details blended into the background, and for that, the padre was thankful.

He did not listen for ghosts. He did not look for phantoms. He did not see or hear anything, except the woman with the keys jingling in her hands, and her footsteps as she led him deeper into the great hall.

"This way," she told him, and she guided him to a place where two sideboards and a buffet cabinet were stationed. One had been knocked over; it was close to the nearest window—which had not been secured any better than the ones in the great hall. The window had broken, and part of a tree had collapsed inside, tearing down a curtain, breaking a table, and disrupting everything else within its reach.

Glass crunched beneath their shoes as Mrs. Alvarez opened the drawers and cabinets, collecting bottles in her arms, and then in her apron. "I don't see the carts, do you?" she asked. "There is one for tea, and one for spirits. I'd take either one of them, right now."

The padre didn't see them. They might have been beneath the curtain, or they may have been sucked outside. Without better light, it was hard to say. "Give me some bottles, I can help carry them," he said, crooking his elbow and offering his free arm.

She held up some brandy in a crystal decanter, still intact despite the tree and the tempest, and reached inside for whatever was next—anything that hadn't broken, and might keep people gently drunk and quiet.

But then they heard a heavy *thunk*.

And then they heard voices back in the lobby.

Forgetting the brandy, and forgetting even that he was holding the only light source, the padre darted to the dining hall's entrance, where a fresh breeze on his face told him something was wrong, and yes—back in the lobby the main doors were wide ajar...their heavy bracing beam discarded like a matchstick on the ground.

"What happened?" he called.

"Vaughn!" the Ranger snarled. "I'm going after him!"

"How did he...?" he meant the brace, lying on its side. Too heavy for one man to lift.

Sister Eileen said, "No one knows. No one saw it. It was there, and then it wasn't—and Vaughn was gone!"

In the dining area, Mrs. Alvarez called anxiously for help. "Don't leave me alone! I can't see!" she cried.

The padre looked at the open doors, and the calm, featureless dark beyond them. He came to a decision.

Handing his candle to the Ranger, he said, "I'll get Vaughn. You see to Mrs. Alvarez—and *watch these people.* Do not let them leave, not for any reason. If I'm not back when the storm begins again, help them close the doors."

Sister Eileen began to object, but he interrupted before she could mount her protest. "You knew when you brought me here. This is what I'm for."

He tossed a nod of his head at the Ranger, who took a deep breath but didn't fight him on it. The old man said, "You're younger and faster. Go get that son of a bitch and bring him back so I can pistol-whip him."

Out the door the padre ran—straight into the cool, calm nothing of almost-midnight.

THE PADRE OPENED HIS EYES, and he looked.

Instead of nothing, brightened only by flashes of distant lightning for instants at a time, he saw outlines... shapes...motion.

The broken, dangling limbs of trees; the hulking shadow of the Jacaranda with its front doors open behind him, and faint candlelight burning within; drag-marks on the ground where the storm-surge had pushed timber, glass, rocks, bricks, fences, fish, shells, sand, crabs, railroad ties, doors, shingles, and God-alone-knew-what-else onto the shore and over it.

The road was gone, nothing left but a muddy mess where not even ruts remained. The walkways around the hotel were likewise washed over with muck, or broken and carried away. But there were footprints, squished into the wet and treacherous ground.

And there was a breathless rushing noise, the sound of someone running in the dark—fumbling, tripping, and climbing up to run again.

Cherie Priest

Frederick Vaughn was drunk as hell and not running very fast, so he was almost easy to catch—almost simple to approach, to seize, and to drag to the ground. The padre caught him like a wolf on a deer, bringing him to his knees in the mud and rolling him onto his back.

"Let me go!" the fugitive demanded, thrashing his head back and forth.

"No! This is madness!"

"Staying *inside* that place is madness! *Actual* madness!" Vaughn objected. "I'm going mad as a hatter...madder than that, listening to that godawful voice, in that godawful lobby. You trapped us in there with it—it was all your idea!"

"It is our only chance to survive the storm! And what do you mean, the voice in the lobby?"

Vaughn writhed feebly on the ground, pinned there by the padre's knees. "You know good and well what I mean! Everyone knows, now. *Everyone* can hear it...that's what it told me." He gave up and collapsed back into the mud. "Maybe everyone else can stand it, maybe it doesn't make their skull itch, like it makes mine itch. Maybe it doesn't bother them, and if that's so, I'm happy for them," he said, without sounding happy at all. "Why did you follow me...how did you even...how did you *see* me? How did you...did you find me?"

Before the padre could respond, Vaughn turned his face aside and vomited whiskey, bile, and water.

The padre sighed, and climbed up—offering Vaughn his hand. "Come, I'll help you. I know the hotel is speaking, but we must get back inside. Only for another few hours," he promised, having no idea how much longer the storm would last, but he would've said anything to hurry the drunk man along. "If we all stay together, and if we can keep the hotel secured, the storm will pass over us soon enough. I'll help you leave, in the morning. Please, come with me."

"I don't know…if I…if I can. I'm sorry, it was stupid…it was so stupid," Vaughn mumbled, staggering to his feet with the padre's help. "I'm sorry. I've been so goddamn *stupid*."

"You're not stupid; you're afraid, like everyone else. No one wants to stay, but do you feel it?" the padre asked, turning his head up to the sky. The stars were out, clear and bright, but to the south a blanket of clouds was drawing up fast—and the breeze was getting its momentum back. "Look, over there: It's the other side of the storm, and it's coming for us. Out here, you'll be dead in an hour. Inside the hotel, you have a chance."

"Do I? Do any of us?" he shook his head, and leaned against the padre as they walked. "I think we used up all our chances. I think we're done for, now. Same as this whole island, and everyone on it."

Juan Rios kept his eyes open, and kept looking. The stars were very bright, and he had the ridiculous idea that they were flaring in protest—determined to burn through the coming clouds and shine on regardless. But the eye was passing over them, and every minute that went by, every step they took, the leaves rustled harder in the trees and the seabirds called out to one another with greater and greater alarm.

"None of us will see the morning," the drunk man mumbled.

The padre adjusted his grip on Vaughn, who kept trying to slide to the ground. "Did the hotel say that?"

"It said a lot of things."

"Then tell me about them," he urged. He wanted to know, and he wanted to keep Frederick Vaughn awake and walking; he wasn't sure if he had the strength to carry him, should he pass out. Besides, it might mean something—did the gaping maw on the lobby floor have the same message for each listener? Or did it craft a new lie for every ear?

"The hotel says…it says that it wants to be free. It will destroy itself to free itself…and it wants to open the windows and doors. It wants the storm to take it."

The padre frowned. "I don't understand."

"It's…concentrated, Father. Don't you see? It's…it's collected enough evil, enough filthy souls like ours…it wants to be swept off its foundations, and scattered to the four winds. Like…like a goddamn dandelion puff," he concluded, then he wretched, and rallied. "Like a goddamn dandelion puff with a thousand seeds, spinning in the air. Blown loose by the storm."

The sick feeling in the pit of the padre's stomach suggested that there was something true to the man's inebriated ramblings. There was something right about it, maybe not *exactly* right, but right enough that he needed to pay attention.

He needed to think about it.

He wanted a word with Sister Eileen and Ranger Korman, and he intended to have one when they returned to the lobby.

But back at the hotel, he sensed more trouble before he saw it.

When he looked, he caught the flicker of candles being moved, carried from place to place in a frantic hunt—or an effort to preserve them. When he listened he heard shouts—threats and warnings, and an appeal from the nun that he couldn't quite hear.

"Hurry," he told Vaughn, but Vaughn stumbled and fell— so he picked him up under one arm and half dragged him, half encouraged him, back to the landing where the doors gaped wide and there was pandemonium on the other side.

The padre was exhausted from the run and from lugging Frederick Vaughn, so he flung the drunk man into the lobby and yanked the doors shut. Finished with him for the moment, Juan Rios stepped over the fellow's moaning form and asked the room at large: "What has happened here?"

Valeria Alvarez was in hysterics, cowering away from the nun while her mother swore and prayed in Spanish—"She's a monster, she's a monster. You didn't tell us she was a monster, you should've said something!" She made the sign of the cross again and again, but the nun did not seem impressed.

Meanwhile, Violetta screamed her own set of unrelated horrors: "I saw Sarah, I saw her! She was here, and she said that I should come! She said to open the doors—she told me she needs me! You have to let me go, let me help her!"

Sister Eileen, coolly apathetic toward the Alvarez women, said only, "Sarah is dead, and you'll stay here...unless you want to follow her into the grave."

"I don't care!" Violetta shrieked. "I have to do what she says—I have to do what they tell me!"

"They?" the padre asked, but no one answered him.

Mrs. Alvarez kept praying, Valeria kept crying, and the McCoy brothers were increasingly agitated by the whole thing— George even called for someone to shut her up.

"I tried," said the nun. "It didn't work."

The Ranger held up his hands and spoke with the loud, low voice of authority. "We're all at our wits end, but we've got to behave ourselves like civilized men! All of you, calm down, for Christ's sake! Listen, can't you hear it out there? The storm is kicking up again—Sister Eileen was right, and now we're in for the second act!"

While he spoke, the padre looked more closely at Mrs. Alvarez and Valeria, and he saw that they were bleeding. The girl's hand was badly torn, and so was her mother's forearm. He thought at first that it was an injury from the beam, fall- ing from the door—or some new trick played by the hotel— which injured whoever it could, whenever it could, however it chose. But the injuries had the ragged, vicious look of a big dog's bite...something with the jaws of a wolf. Something that

Cherie Priest

didn't just bite, but chomped and pulled, and tore flesh away in chunks.

The padre looked at the nun, still facing down the other women—daring them to challenge her again. They were cowed, or at least the mother was. Valeria was out of her mind with something...grief? Despair? Confusion?

He scanned the rest of the lobby, wondering if anyone there had any medical training, but the nun's touch on his arm startled his attention back to her. "She'll be fine," she told him. "It looks worse than it is. Her mother will wrap it up, when she calms down."

"If you're certain…"

"Oh, I am. But she's positive she heard Sarah calling out, so she opened the east wing fire door."

"Has anyone else gone through it?"

She shook her head. "I don't think so. The Ranger watched it, while I watched everyone else. Go close it, if you would. The storm isn't upon us yet—but it will be soon. I don't know if the place can withstand another round or not; but if the fire doors fail us, it will all come down around our ears."

"And we'll all be swept out to sea, scattered like the seeds of a dandelion."

She regarded him with curiosity. "Something's given you an idea?"

"A bad idea," he told her. "It was Vaughn, something he said out there. But I'll go…I'll take a look around the east wing. I'll see if there's anything left of Sarah to wander."

"You think there might be?"

He did not mention that he'd seen Constance Fields, or that the whirlpool spiral on the lobby floor had spoken—to him, and to others. He almost asked if it'd spoken to the nun, too, but there wasn't time. The breeze was no longer a breeze; it had become wind once more. Its strength was growing, and the distant thunder was less distant with every tick of the wall clock, closer and more forceful. It was rolling in on top of them.

All the padre said was, "Yes, there might be something left of Sarah. If so, I will shut her out. I won't be long."

The Ranger asked if he needed any help.

"Yes, I need someone to stay here, and make sure those doors stay shut, this time. David, George—put the beam back against them. I don't think Vaughn will try to escape again," he said of the now-unconscious man on the floor, lying in a puddle of his own vomit. "But someone else might." His eyes narrowed toward the Alvarez mother and daughter—and then to Violetta, who had not joined them, but she still stared with awe and a touch of horror at the nun, who declined to address their fears.

"Go on, if you're going," Sister Eileen said.

So he went—the same admonition as before: "If I'm not back when the storm sets in again, you must shut the fire door and leave me out there."

Down a short corridor that led to the east wing, the fire door lever had been drawn down—and the door was hanging open. Not widely open, but ajar by about a foot...that was as far as the girl had cranked it back, before the nun had caught up to her.

(Did Sister Eileen bite her? Had she left those awful injuries on the Alvarez women? Perhaps he did not want to know. Maybe he would not ask.)

He slipped inside, into the darkened hallway without a hint of light. He hadn't brought a candle. He had a feeling he wouldn't need it—not when he could still look, and still listen. Besides, if Sarah was there, he trusted her to come and find him, just like Constance Fields.

He closed his eyes. Exhaled. Opened them again.

"Sarah?" he called quietly. His voice bounced back and forth between the walls, the ceiling, and all the closed doors. Again he could see outlines and shapes, not quite glowing around the edges, but discernable all the same. Behind him, there was still a little faint light from the lobby, peeking around the edge of the fire barrier...but it wasn't enough to help him.

Only God could help him now, or the Mother, if she chose to.

"Sarah, are you here?"

Beside him, sharp and sad: *Yes.*

She was very close, and so he could see her a little, mostly in shades of gray and white, the contrast muddled in the dark, and in her death. Her eyes were empty and black, and her neck was crooked—her head held off to the right, and the sight of her was all the more jarring because of the angle.

He couldn't meet her gaze, not really. Not like that.

He wanted to jump back away from her, but he planted his feet on the rug and tried to steady his breathing, to keep the fear tamped down. But if he'd ever been *tempted* to run screaming away in fright, surely this was the time—when the yellow-haired dead thing in a night dress lolled its head to one side, and then the other, loose as a wheel on a broken axle.

He swallowed hard, forcing himself to hold his ground. "Sarah, you stayed."

I should have left, because I could have left. But I was so afraid, Father. And when I did this, she gestured toward her neck with one long, white hand. *I broke the only vow I'd ever made. The only one that meant anything.*

"But...between us, the sister and I...we thought the hotel had killed you—like it killed Constance Fields, and the people before her."

She shook her head sadly, or she tried. It swayed back and forth, her neck rolling around her shoulder and back again.

Until I took my own life, the hotel had nothing to keep me with. Now it makes me stay. Now it has that power. Look at me. Look at my choices, and look at what I've done. Look at what I've undone.

"You left Tim..." he said thoughtfully. And then, with a sudden shock of absolute panic. "Oh God, where *is* Tim? Is he dead too? I haven't seen him since he gave you the doll!"

Nor have I, she said, sounding as sad and confused as when she was alive. *But he is not dead, or else, I think...I think I would know. I think he'd come to me. The hotel doesn't need for us to be alone, it just needs for us to serve.*

At the back of the hall, toward the rear exit all barricaded shut, he heard something click, shift, and pop.

"What was that?"

We can only serve.

"We?"

Emily is here too. She never left—I don't know how, or why.

"Miss Nowell is dead, too?"

She also serves, yes.

"You keep saying that—but what do you mean? What does the hotel want from you? Why does it collect you here, and keep you here even after death?"

She sighed, long and low and slow. It was almost the sound of air leaving a corpse, a last breath drawn out for posterity. Behind her, another series of noises, in another room down the hall.

We have to open it up. That's what it wants—it wants to let the storm inside. The hotel and the storm...they're working together. Two sides of the same penny, you understand? As above, so below. Isn't that how they put it?

"That is how the devil put it." His voice was dry, and his ears still picked up the commotion, room by room. Outside, the wind was rising, and the rain was coming again—in fits and starts, but it'd be worse by a thousand-fold soon enough.

I'm sorry, she said. Her broken, lopsided form retreated... skating slowly away, and growing fainter by the foot. *You tried to help, and you couldn't.*

"That's not true," he insisted. "I can still help—I can still stop this!"

I'm sorry. But it's coming around again.

She was gone, vanished as if she'd never been there in the first place.

"Wait, no!"

The hotel replied with a shocking explosion—as every door on the floor flew open at once, smashing against the walls and letting in a dozen gusts of ocean-smelling air. The doors banged and flapped, and he knew without looking that likewise every window was open in every room. A sickening, rising pitch to the wind announced that his time was nearly up, as surely as the first-floor hallway was compromised...

...and the floor above it, he was sure.

Upstairs more doors yawned and smacked in the gusty hallway over his head, and he could only pray that the other fire doors had not been touched.

And he could run.

That was the other thing, and it was the only thing—before he was shut out in the lost corridor and the storm took him, too.

5

THE PADRE RETURNED TO THE lobby, entering beneath the stairs just as the raindrops fell like hammers, battering the big doors and windows, rattling the nerves of everyone still trapped there, in the center. All eyes turned to him, and all candles flickered together in sympathy; but the lights held, and he told himself that it was a good sign— that if the light could hold, it might make a difference and the building might hold.

Or at least the center.

"I've closed the fire door," he said, and he did not care for the shaky sound of his words. He cleared his throat and added, a little stronger, "But the east wing is probably lost. The doors and windows are open, and the storm has come inside."

The Ranger swore and nibbled at a cigarette. He picked up a candle, lit the edge of the papers, and sucked it until a hard red coal burned on the end. "Who the hell would do a thing like that?"

Cherie Priest

"It was Sarah, and Emily Nowell. The hotel has taken them both, and now they serve it. I don't know how much power they have—I don't know how much help they need—but the Jacaranda wants them to fling it all open. The hotel wants to meet the storm, and be carried away by it."

"You don't know that!" Mrs. Anderson shrieked, and when her husband tried to sooth her with a hand upon her arm, she turned to him and said, "He doesn't know that! The hotel will stand, just fine!"

"Not the east wing. But the north wing might, and the center is still sound. We must keep the faith, and keep the fire doors secured...and have faith that the hotel can stand. It *will* stand. And in the morning, we will be standing too."

No one questioned anything else he said, though he couldn't imagine that anyone believed every word of it. If it was true, that everyone knew about all the deaths, and no one ever spoke of it...well, no one was speaking of it now, either. No one called him a maniac for suggesting that two dead women were trying to sabotage everyone else's survival efforts; no one challenged his assertion that the hotel had a plan for itself.

The room only fell into something like silence—as close to silence as it could fall, considering the pelting rain and the revival of the thunder outside.

The storm cracked and rolled, shaking the lobby and threatening the candles, and the compromised east wing whistled like a flute. Glass broke and doors creaked, curtains flapped and were sucked out into the night. The building groaned, and another piece of roof peeled away with a hard, loud series of pops that let in more wind, more water.

"This will be the worst of it," the nun promised him. He hadn't realized she was standing right beside him, having left the Alvarez women to collapse together, crying with or without her presence.

"How do you mean?"

"The eye of the storm—the walls around it, that's where the storm is strongest. If we survive the next hour, we'll survive the night. I'm sure of it."

"I'll do my best to believe you. Tell me, Sister: do you know what became of Tim?"

A look of horror crossed her face. "No!" she gasped quietly, taking him by the hand and drawing him closer, so that she might whisper the rest. "Good God, where could he have gone? I haven't seen him since he left Sarah's room, and he wasn't anywhere in the hotel before we closed it. We searched! Everyone searched!"

"Let us hope," he whispered back to her, "that the boy evacuated with everyone else. No one has seen him, not even his cousin's ghost. There's nothing we can do for him now except pray for his safety, wherever he is."

She nodded and sighed, and the Ranger joined them, with a cigarette gripping the corner of his mouth.

He reported, "No one's turning on anybody, yet. That's not much, but it's something."

The nun gazed from face to face, taking stock of those who remained. She said, "Let us hope it remains that way. Tonight, the battles must all be waged against the hotel, and not against one another."

Juan Rios checked over his shoulder, where the lovely, terrible mosaic turned (or did not turn) on the floor between the staircase landings. "Vaughn said the hotel speaks to everyone, now, and Sarah's spirit suggested the same thing. Has it spoken to either of you?"

"I don't know..." said the Texan slowly. "I've heard a voice, once or twice. Wasn't sure what to make of it. Couldn't understand it very well—something about the storm. Something about the ocean."

The nun agreed, "It has spoken to me, but…it's as if someone is whispering on the other side of a closed door. I can't understand what it says, or what it wants."

"Maybe it's time to try speaking, rather than listening. We've asked our questions of everyone else; why not ask the hotel itself?"

The nun and the Ranger looked at the padre with surprise, and no small bit of concern.

"Do you really think that's a good idea?" asked Korman. "In my experience, when something nasty starts talking…the best thing you can do is plug your ears. These things lie, padre."

"But even a lie is an answer," he argued. "What else do we have, right now? Nothing but time, and apparently the hotel likes to talk. Let's give it an audience, and see what it wants to say. Even if it's nonsense, or some devious falsehood, it might be worth hearing."

They decided to speak with it together, just the three of them.

The other men and women in the lobby were comfortably oblivious; they kept near the front of the large, lovely room, close to the doors and closer to the collection of candles—now burning lower, but augmented by the few Mrs. Alvarez had ultimately scavenged from the dining hall.

If anyone heard what the trio was up to, no one paid attention.

Perhaps no one cared.

The nun, the padre, and the Ranger approached the mosaic on the floor.

They stood at its edges and stared down at the swirled pattern, and now the padre thought that it did not merely spin, when he looked away. It also *grew*. The day he'd arrived, it'd been a patch between the staircase landings. Now it almost bridged the distance between them.

He did not mention this to his companions. They'd probably noticed it already, and if they hadn't, there was no sense in pointing it out. So the thing was growing, swelling in strength and size. Why shouldn't it? The storm above was calling to it at least, and the dead were feeding it, at worst.

One hungry vortex calling to another. One great evil feeding another.

He shook those thoughts away. They weren't helpful.

Maybe the Jacaranda wouldn't be helpful either, but it was worth trying. Anything was, when the storm's eye-wall hammered the exposed east wing—tugging at the floors, picking them apart and whisking them away.

So he stood at the edge as if it were a pool, and he might dip his toes in it.

Looking down into the thing now, seeing it and knowing what it had done, and what it must be capable of...it did not seem like merely a pretty pattern on a lobby floor. It was so much more than a design made out of ceramic squares; it was a hole in the world, and he might fall in—should he lean too close. The vertigo shook him, left him with a dry mouth and a low, thrumming sense of anger that he couldn't quite place. He didn't know if the anger was his, or if it belonged to the hotel.

So he asked it: "What do you want?" He cast the question into the hole, sending it all the way down to hell—if that's where it went.

He steeled himself and he Looked down into the spiral. He Listened for its response.

The world shifted, the floor moved beneath him.

I want what everything wants—to be free, and to be strong. I want to grow.

The directness of the answer startled him, but almost any reply would have. He felt strange—off-kilter, drunk, or sick. It could have been simple proximity, or it could've been some

Cherie Priest

change in the air pressure, brought about by the storm. It didn't matter. He was dizzy, and his face was hot.

"Did you hear that?" he asked the other two.

Sister Eileen said, "I heard...something. But you caught it clearly?"

He nodded, and wished he hadn't. His head was full of springs, coiled too tightly. So he asked the vortex another question, the only other one he could think of. He asked it in Spanish, because neither of his companions understood the language—and if the hotel wished to speak to him alone, then he would speak alone to the hotel.

"What are you?"

To his surprise, it answered this one, too.

It answered him at length, and with what felt like honesty, but might have been nothing more than a fairy tale.

Like everything else, it began with a tree.

Hundreds of years ago—but you've heard that part. A monument planted in sorrow, watered with tears, and it grew, and grew, and grew...its roots went down and its branches went up. While its branches reached only the sky, in time the roots reached someplace much farther away.

Beneath your feet lies something very old, very vast. Something bigger than you can imagine, and more ancient than Christ, but your Bible does mention it, in passing. Your Good Book gave the old thing a name: It called the beast "Leviathan."

Now it sleeps beneath you—beneath the island, even beneath the ocean. It sleeps and it dreams, the old thing so great that its heart beats only once in a hundred years.

The roots of the jacaranda tree reached all the way down to its resting place, drawn there by the tears and all the small griefs that were brought to it, over the ages. All the lovers ever parted by death came to this tree and told it their stories, and they fed it their tears; every mother who lost a baby; every father who lost a son in war; every orphan alone on the face of the earth, did bring his sadness to this tree. So in time, the roots went very deep indeed.

For like calls to like, does it not? One small bit of sorrow finds other sorrow, and comforts itself. Feeds itself. And so it grows.

Now imagine, if you can, the woe of the ages...of an exile coiled beneath the big round Gulf, dreaming of waking and seeing the stars again—watching them spin overhead, and seeing the other great spirals in the sky above, all of them spinning like the whirlpool, these distant places in heaven where everything spins and spins and spins.

Heaven and earth both turn, Father. And so does hell.

The padre's mouth was very dry...he would've taken any drop of water, or any sip of spirits either—except that it would mean leaving the vortex, and not hearing the heavy, buzzing, humming low voice explain itself.

(If indeed that's what it was doing, when it might have only been spinning a lie.)

As far as he could tell, the nun and the Ranger heard none of this—or if they did, they understood precious little. It was hurting him to listen so hard, but he couldn't stop now, not when he had it talking. Not when it had him listening.

"The deaths you've caused, they feed you like the tears fed the tree—is that right? You're a carnivorous thing, at heart."

You also grow stronger when you consume. How is it different?

"You're feeding on...on lives. On people, and their souls."

No one here, who has ever come or gone, has been innocent. Grant that much, at least. Grant us that there is a pattern, and that it has been served by the very worst—by men and women who have cheated, lied, and broken holy vows. Like yourself, and like the Ranger.

He flashed a quick look at the nun. Her eyes were closed.

The hotel explained, *Her vows were merely bent, not broken. She cannot be held here, but still she chooses to stay.*

Still in Spanish, still trusting that no one within earshot understood, he whispered: "What is she?"

She is afflicted, it said, but offered nothing else.

The padre thought about pressing the matter, but the storm was directly overhead—prying bricks loose and throwing them, pulling doors off hinges down in the open wing, and tossing them like skipping stones into the night. Time was not on his side.

And why should it be? Almost nothing else was.

Tonight—and very soon—the storm will have its way, and I will have mine. I will rise up into the air and break apart. I will become a million pieces, a million seeds scattered to the winds...and winds like these can hurl me a very great distance. I will have Texas, and Louisiana, and the old Spanish states to the east. I will take the coasts and the mountains of Mexico, to the west. I am one, but I will be many. You will call me Legion, because that's what your holy testaments called me.

This structure above me will fall, and you will fall with it. But I will rise.

"Padre? Padre? *Father.*"

Sister Eileen was immediately before him, standing on the mosaic—her small feet atop the edges, and it looked like she stood on a sheet of glass above a cavern. That's what the padre noticed when he shook off the listening, and the looking. He noticed that he was on his hands and knees; he noticed how little her shoes were, and how they appeared to stand on nothing but thin air, but that was only a trick of the hotel, the terrible mirage of its voice.

"Sister," he muttered. His head was still full of springs, a clock that was over-wound and on the verge of breaking. But he heard her, he saw her, and the vortex wasn't speaking anymore. Sister Eileen was.

Relief was written all over her face, and more than a little fear, too. "I thought we'd lost you for a minute, there. Get up, and come around. We have a problem."

He could hear it, now that she said it: over near the front doors, an argument. "What's happening?"

"Cabin fever?" She gave him her hand and helped pull him up. "They don't know how to fight the hotel, so now they fight each other."

"I had my hopes, but it was bound to happen," the Ranger said unhappily, as he set off for the fray.

At first, Juan Rios tried to avoid the mosaic as he staggered upright, then he gave up. The pattern was bigger now, even bigger than before. It didn't just touch both staircase landings… it slipped underneath them. The padre couldn't shake the sick, weird feeling that the thing had been feeding on him, even as it spoke to him.

He collected himself, tried not to lean on the nun, and rejoined the group out by the doors—just in time to catch a fight between the McCoy brothers and Ranger Korman.

"Both of you, sit yourselves down!" the old Texan ordered.

"But we *heard* him," George insisted. "And David saw him! You've got to let us check, at least—you can't just leave him locked out there, to die!"

"Who, Tim?" the padre asked, still trying to get his head around the situation.

"Oh no...where *is* Tim? Has anyone seen him?" asked Violetta, but the nun quieted her with a look before too many other voices could add to the query.

"It was Matthew," George said. "Our brother, he's here. He came here to meet us..."

Exasperated, and still finding his feet—still shaking the wool and the cogs and the springs from his head—the padre said, "Your brother Matthew is dead. You told us that already."

"But he's not!" David swore. "He told us, it was a mistake! He's here—he's stuck on the north wing, on the other side of the door!"

The Ranger had drawn his gun. "It's the *hotel*, you damn fool. It's lying to you, same as it lied to that girl over there, and same as it lies to everyone. Now sit yourself down, and *nobody* is opening that door, do you hear me?"

Outside, the storm begged to differ.

They could all hear it, and those who weren't watching the human drama unfold were looking up anxiously toward the ceiling, listening and wondering if everything would hold after all. They'd told themselves over and over that of *course* the place would stand, and of *course* it would weather the hurricane—but all those promises they'd made to themselves didn't mean much when the wind was ripping away tiles, yanking loose the sub-roofing, picking up furniture from the top floors and throwing it into the ocean like a spoiled child tearing down a dollhouse.

Sister Eileen whispered, "Father, do you still have those guns?"

"No." It would've been more honest to say he didn't have them presently, for they were in his bag upstairs. He always carried them, even if he never used them. Without temptation, there was no virtue in resistance.

Or it might've just been that he liked them, and he didn't want to let them go.

And dear God, he wished he had them in his hands right that moment—when the Ranger was trying to keep the situation managed, and Valeria Alvarez was crying, and her mother was yelling at the McCoy brothers to sit down, and David McCoy was standing behind his brother, reaching into his jacket.

There was no time to shout, not even that small space to take a breath and let it out with a warning...when David retrieved a six-shooter and drew it and fired it, and then the women were screaming and even Frederick Vaughn was awake and shouting unintelligibly, and no one knew where the next bullet would fall, or who it would hit.

No.
That wasn't what happened.

The moment froze. The Ranger was the one who'd fired, and his shot had been true—not through the heart, because George was in the way; but through the shoulder, and David toppled backward onto the sofa where he'd been playing cards.

The gun was still in his hand, and then it wasn't.

George called his brother's name, and turned to help him— no, he turned to take the gun away—but the Ranger was faster than him, too. He didn't shoot. There was time for a warning, just this once.

"Boy, I swear to God you point that thing at me and it'll be the last stupid thing you ever do. Hold it up..." he urged. He was all lawman, and no one in the room budged to intervene. No one spoke, no one moved. Only the driving rain, the tearing, rending, shredding wind against the hotel broke up the quiet that had fallen in the wake of that shot.

George didn't move. He was fixed, the gun in his hand but aimed at the ceiling, or at no place in particular. He stared down at his brother, gasping and fretting, maybe dying—or maybe not.

"Hold it by the handle, just two fingers, and put it down on the table," the Ranger instructed more precisely.

"It's Matthew," he breathed. "I know it was him, and they shut him out."

"You're not an idiot, you're just wrong. This place, boy—it does things to people's heads, you know that now. Everybody knows it. You think you owe your brother something, and that's your weak spot. That's what it pokes with a stick, trying to make you do something that'll get you killed. It likes to see us fighting, you know that, don't you? It likes to see us kill each other. It saves it the trouble."

The padre stepped up slowly, his hands aloft to show he was unarmed—and had no plans to join the fray. "If you die here, the hotel can use you. It turns you into a servant, that's what Sarah told me."

George looked like he wanted to spit at something, but he didn't. He just hovered there, above David. Gun still in hand, still directionless. "Oh, for chrissake—what would that yellow-haired girl know about it, anyway?"

The Ranger answered him: "She's dead, that's what she'd know about it. Hadn't you figured that out by now? Everyone who ain't standing here, right in this room, right now…everyone else is dead."

"The hotel's picked up quite a staff by now," the nun mused, her eyes wandering toward the awful sounds above them, where the east wing was coming apart, board by board and brick by brick. There was no more glass breaking, not anymore. It'd all been pulled free and cast out into the night.

The padre couldn't argue with her there. "They're tearing the place apart at the seams, opening all the doors and windows. I don't know why they can't open the fire doors."

"That *is* an excellent question," the nun mused. "I wonder why that is…"

George hesitated, his arm drooping from the weight of the gun, and with uncertainty about how he was going to use it.

"George," Sister Eileen said gently. "We have bigger problems, right now. You have to leave the doors shut, and you have to put the gun down. Let me look at your brother. I'll clean him up and bandage him."

But Mrs. Alvarez screamed, "Don't let her near him! She's a monster! She won't help him, she'll eat him alive!"

Everyone turned to look at the frantic woman, out of pure surprise.

Even the Ranger turned to look, and he shouldn't have.

George raised the gun, and hardly aimed it. He pointed it, that was all—and he pulled the trigger twice. A third time. And he would've gone for a fourth except that something stopped him, a blur of motion shaped like the nun, more or less. She was on him before anyone could or cry out, or gasp.

The padre ran to Horatio Korman.

One bullet had blown his hat off. One had caught him in the temple, and then it was over before he hit the ground.

He didn't hit it immediately, but joint by joint, he folded. He fell. He didn't drop the gun, but he didn't fire it, either. His hand lay beside his hip and the empty holster, a solid grip still lingering on the piece.

The padre gently pried his fingers free, and slipped the weapon into his own hand, and then into the pocket of his cassock. He said a fast, breathless prayer in Spanish and closed the Ranger's eyes, then retrieved the old man's hat and placed it across his face.

That's how fast it'd happened.

Faster than a blink.

When Juan Rios finished his prayer and sat up, he was struck by the sudden feeling that he wasn't alone now—and that was ridiculous, because of course he wasn't alone. The stunned bystanders scarcely breathed, scarcely cried. They were as silent as a photograph, so it was something else he heard...at the very edge of his senses, just under the rampaging noise of the storm outside. Something else wanted his attention.

He exhaled, and listened.

He heard only the rain and the trembling sky.

He listened again.

Violetta was behind the counter with her mother and sister; Frederick Vaughn cowered behind one of the sofas; the Andersons clutched one another on the floor beneath the coffee table; and one by one, or two by two, everyone had taken cover except for David McCoy, who had passed out from the bleeding.

He wondered where Sister Eileen was, and like magic, she stood up to reveal herself. She'd tackled George to the floor and rendered him either unconscious or restrained—he didn't know which, because he couldn't see him. Two of the candles had been knocked over and extinguished, and a third was guttering.

The light was all but gone. The Ranger was dead.

And overhead, the storm was not finished yet—it had not quite given up on its prey, and the hotel was not yet satisfied that it must stay put on Galveston Island. But when the padre listened he heard beyond the ruined wings and the barricaded doors that some peak had been passed, and the hurricane's power waned.

The raindrops were only as big as grapes, and the thunder was only loud enough to make his teeth shake. The lightning came only twice a minute, and the seething, screaming wind had lost its highest notes.

"It isn't over," the nun whispered.

Juan Rios Looked at her. He saw eyes that were as round and gold as doubloons from a galleon, and he saw a shadow of a shape—an outline around her that looked in profile like it was not human, though it might have been once. He recognized the shape, and crossed himself. He understood what the vortex had meant by "afflicted," and he marveled at her tenacity...and wondered if he ought to.

She was not even breathing hard, and there was blood on her hands. Perfectly ordinary hands, dainty like her feet. Petite, like that small bow of a mouth with just a smudge of dried blood left beside it on her jaw.

"It isn't over," she said again.

"But it *will* be. The hotel will stand until morning. The storm was not enough, but *we* were."

"And those doors. Something about them..."

An enormous crack of thunder assured them that the hurricane had life in it yet, but the next roll suggested that it was moving along all the same. Everything dimmed by bits and pieces, by a quieter howl to the maelstrom...by less and less rain, clattering against the windows that remained.

It dimmed into the silence that eventually followed, after the last candle had burned down to a puddle and a piece of ash.

Part Five

The Morning

By DAWN, IT WAS ONLY raining.

Without a word, without opening the fire doors to return to their room or collect any of their belongings, the survivors unbraced the entrance doors and left for the ferries, or for the Strand—if any of it still remained. There was no chatter of plans, no whispering about the police, and no idle questions about what would become of the hotel now.

No one cared. All anyone wanted to do was escape, and when the sun came up, everyone who was still alive...did.

The padre and the nun remained behind long enough to close and lock the front doors behind themselves; and using some paint they'd found in a storage closet, they scrawled a great warning across them: CHOLERA, KEEP OUT.

You could always find cholera, or typhoid, or any number of similar illnesses in the wake of a storm like that one. No one would question the message, and it was more likely to keep curiosity seekers away than any mere admonition against trespassing, or a declaration that the building had been condemned.

And it *was* condemned. Not in any official sense, but heaven only knew how long it would take for word to reach the building's owners. They were all somewhere deep in the heart of Texas, the padre assumed...and he had no plans to leave the Jacaranda Hotel standing long enough for anyone to claim or restore it. He'd made up his mind, and the nun agreed with him.

But the island needed to dry out first.

For a full week after the storm, the padre and the nun waited at the convent—which yes, remained standing, and fairly unscathed. They tended to the injured, composed letters, sent telegrams, and made themselves as quietly helpful as innocent, ordinary people might be.

And then they went back.

In the light of day, without any rain, it was clear that the Jacaranda had sustained terrible damage from the hurricane. The east wing was all but lost, and the north wing was missing its top floor. The bottom two floors might collapse in on themselves at any moment, or then again, they might not.

But the center had held, as everyone had prayed and promised.

The nun unlocked the great doubled doors, using the keys Mrs. Alvarez had left behind—not remembering she'd ever had them, or wondering what had become of them. Everything had been so foggy, in those first hours afterward. Everything was abandoned, even things that once had seemed important.

Like the hotel itself, tomb that it was.

It had been too wet to dig any more graves, so the nun and the padre had left the McCoy brothers where they were, and wrapped Ranger Korman in some blankets—then placed him in the dining hall. It didn't seem right to leave him there in the lobby with the others, or with the terrible pattern on the floor, that swelling, hungry maw that would eat the whole world if they fed it long enough.

It didn't make much sense, but it felt like the right thing to do.

Even with the front doors open, the lobby was bleak and dark. It smelled like rotting wood, wet rugs, and old blood. And it absolutely reeked of death.

The McCoy brothers were stacked on the far sofa, their lifeless limbs free of the rigor that held them taut for a while—and now they settled into a slumped puddle of parts that were drawing flies and rats. When the nun approached the bodies, she covered her nose and mouth with her sleeve, shook her head, and crossed herself.

"You aren't going to bury them, are you?"

"I had not planned on it. The Ranger, though. He deserves a grave. Just in case it matters, I'd rather not leave him inside."

She nodded, and said, "I'll get the shovels out of the cart."

They'd arrived in a small horse-drawn number, loaded with the tools they expected to need. By the time the nun returned, the padre had relocated the Ranger's body to a spot in the garden—not far from where he'd buried Constance Fields, who had mercifully remained underground, despite the flooding.

They dug together, shovels sticking in the muddy earth, moving scoop after scoop. Juan Rios did not comment on the small woman's strength, for she kept pace with him as he jammed the tool down into the muck, and heaved it out again, over and over; both of them flinging the earth in great, dirty arcs that left a ring around the hole.

When they were finished, they held a brief, private service and covered up the Ranger. They did not have a stone, but they improvised a cross with rocks and seashells, and they said their final prayers.

The farewell was brief, but heartfelt.

Their farewell to the hotel was likewise heartfelt, but longer in the making—and much grander in scope.

Back at the cart, where the patient old horse chewed a mouthful of grass it'd nabbed from the lawn, there were three large barrels of kerosene lamp oil and an equally sized container of gunpowder.

"Do you think it will be enough?" the padre wondered.

"I don't see why not. There's water on the top floors, where there are any top floors left…but if we set the center alight, and open the fire doors…if nothing else, the place will collapse. Don't you think?"

"Let's find out."

Carefully, methodically, they splashed and dashed and spread the flammables on every promising surface. Then they released the remaining fire doors, one by one. "I still don't know why they worked," the nun said, cranking the last to a fully open position. "I still can't imagine why they held it all at bay."

"Something about the metal, perhaps," he guessed. "They're very heavy—with these steel sheets for armor. There are a thousand stories about dark things being held back by lead and its kin. For that matter, there are wood beams in the center, beneath the metal. It could be rowan, or some other helpful tree."

"Do your investigations always leave you with so many things unanswered?"

He ran his hand up and down the big door's painted surface.

He Looked, and he Listened. But he felt nothing.

"Yes. As often as not."

"It seems like a shame, doesn't it?" Sister Eileen stood in the lobby, staring up at the elaborate ceiling fans, and over at Violetta's counter, and the system of bells and pulleys behind it that connected room to room—to housekeeping services, and the management, or whoever else a guest might require.

"Not really. The faster this place burns, the happier I'll be."

"Oh, you know what I mean. All this wonderful technology, in this beautiful place. On a beautiful island, at the edge of a beautiful ocean. All of it, turned so ugly. I'll never understand it."

The padre remembered what the hotel had told him. He still hadn't related it to the nun, and probably would never bother. He was still sorting through it all, deciding what had been true and what it meant, if anything. "It isn't our task to understand; it is our task to help, when we are able." He pulled out a box of matches and lifted one to strike it, then paused. "Look, do you see? Something has changed. You can see it in the floor."

The space between the two great staircase landings, where a whirlpool design was figured into the tiles...the design that sometimes grew, and sometimes moved, shifted, when no one was watching...it was not growing anymore, and it was not moving. It was the same size as the first time the padre had seen it, perhaps as long across as he was tall.

"You're right...it looks...ordinary, almost. Does it still speak? Does it still scream?"

He struck the match. "Not to me."

They watched the place burn from a safe distance, across the street and past the lawn that the horse had nibbled upon. The horse was not very impressed by it all. He whinnied and snorted with impatience, not caring for the spectacle in the slightest—and rather wanting to return to his stable.

But the nun and the padre stayed until the last corner had fallen to rubble, and the last beams had been reduced to glimmering coals. The Jacaranda Hotel fell down upon itself and simmered, crackling and popping, floors breaking and windows shattering from the heat.

The hotel did not beg for assistance, or plead for any respite.

Whatever had given it such sinister life was either quiet, or already dead. And no one else came out to watch it burn.

No one came to see it at all, not until another three days had passed, and the ashes were cool enough to touch—the debris charred until it was light as feathers, and easily pushed aside by a big man with a broad back. Three days after the fire, Tim came alone with a shovel, an axe, and a broom. He'd taken them from the gardener's shed, which surely had been destroyed in the storm. Unless it hadn't been.

It took him a full day to find his way to the bottom, to the center.

It took another day to clear away what was left of the brittle, burned stairs and the skeletal wreckage of furniture, lost to the flame. By then, no one could have seen the yellow-straw hair or the freckles on his cheeks. He was covered in ash, from head to toe—the soot had worked itself into the cracks in his skin, and the ashes had filled his mouth, climbed up his nose. He coughed, and he was thirsty. But still he dug through the hotel's remains.

And he found what he was looking for.

Carefully, for the task was delicate, now...he took his broom and swept the old smoke and ceiling tins aside. He scrubbed and scrubbed with its bristles, scraping them into the grooves between the tiles until it was exposed to the air once again— a great whirlpool mosaic, done in tiles of blue and green and black, flecked with white.

It was smaller than he remembered, but things had changed, and that was all right. Things would change again, and that would be all right too. Sarah had told him so, when she'd finally found him the morning after the storm.

Then again, she'd also told him to leave the hotel and go back home to Georgia—and he couldn't do that, could he? No, because he'd made a promise to take care of the place. Not to Sarah, or to the nun, or the Ranger, or the padre. He hadn't made it to Mrs. Alvarez, or anyone else.

He'd made it to the Jacaranda Hotel, and he knew what happened when you broke a promise there.